JUNK BOY

JUNK BOY

TONY ABBOTT

KATHERINE TEGEN BOOKS
An Imprint of HarperCollins Publishers

Katherine Tegen Books is an imprint of HarperCollins Publishers.

Junk Boy

Copyright © 2020 by Tony Abbott

All rights reserved. Printed in the United States of America.
No part of this book may be used or reproduced in any manner
whatsoever without written permission except in the case of brief
quotations embodied in critical articles and reviews. For information
address HarperCollins Children's Books, a division of HarperCollins
Publishers, 195 Broadway, New York, NY 10007.
www.harpercollinschildrens.com

Library of Congress Cataloging-in-Publication Data

Names: Abbott, Tony, author.
Title: Junk boy / Tony Abbott.
Description: First edition. | New York, NY : Katherine Tegen Books,
    an imprint of HarperCollins Publishers, [2020] | Audience: Ages 14
    up. | Audience: Grades 10–12. | Summary: "Bobby, who is bullied
    by the kids at school for living in a home with a front yard that is
    filled with garbage, meets a young artist who teaches him to see
    himself as more than 'Junk Boy.'"— Provided by publisher.
Identifiers: LCCN 2020000858 | ISBN 9780062491251 (hardcover)
Subjects: CYAC: Novels in verse. | Family problems—Fiction. | Child
    abuse—Fiction. | Friendship—Fiction.
Classification: LCC PZ7.5.A23 Ju 2020 | DDC [Fic]—dc23
LC record available at https://lccn.loc.gov/2020000858

Typography by David DeWitt
20 21 22 23 24   PC/LSCH   10 9 8 7 6 5 4 3 2 1

First Edition

To Nora

for faith from the beginning

JUNK
BOY

A Rail Trail

winds far from
any normal street
into the woods

it used to be a flat path
for a train to run on
now it's for people to

the green house there
the dark green house
down
off the end
three miles by foot
from every human road
is where I live

Our House Is Sick

all hours with mice
their little bone claws
scratching on the floor or
in the ceiling
and
their furry up-your-nose smell
when they die
into thumb-sized
little husks

not just inside
outside too
our front steps are cracked
so you have to take
the top two
two at once
I jump them quick
I always have

our house has propane heat
a big tank in the back
but my dad Jimmy's so cheap
sometimes he won't
turn it up because of bills

and since he gives me
almost no money to buy food
we don't have tons around

that plus the mice
get to it first anyway
and eat it in the ceiling
and die and dry up
when it runs out

so

good for them

but
being thin
and cold
and quick to move
all make
me
hard to see

so

good for me

Our Yard Has Junk

moldering all over it
(*moldering*'s from a song
my father listens too much to)

it is
the junk of some life
or bunch of lives
(not mine)

you honestly
could live outside
with all the trash
dumped in the yard out here
from who knows who or when

which (living outside)
because of everything
going and not going
on with me
is something I think
a lot about

Here Is a (Partial) List

stacks of half-chopped wood
planks ripped from
some home improvement
that didn't get improved

five busted chairs, no, six
one overturned washer
two picnic umbrellas
with broken spokes

a kitchen table
whose three remaining legs
jerk up into the air
like some dead cow's
after an accident
with a truck

a plastic baby pool cracked
down the side and filled
with muck and leaves
a battlefield
of empty gallon cans
of paint I never saw
on any wall

three lawn mowers (one push)
piles of sodden blankets
critters and their families
have made a
bathroom of

remains of what might
have been coffee makers
or radios or bomb-makings
(just kidding)
and clocks and busted
farm tools
but from what farm
I sure don't know

a ton of broken blinds and shades
an arsenal of curtain rods
endless end-less
extension cords
the arm of a lounge chair
(just the arm)

a hundred shattered plates
that maybe date
from when my mother
threw them at him

(which might explain
why we have only two
plates left
one for me
and one for him)

parts of three (or more) old cars
a rusted pickup truck
that mostly runs but is so rusted
you could poke a hole
just with your fingertip
through its flaky skin

and a camper
from my mother

an old round-ended
hard-top flat-nose
V-dub camper bus
parked up on cinder blocks
from nineteen sixty-seven
two-tone cream
and powder blue
(that haven't been
cream or blue for years)
that Jimmy says was hers

that someday
I swear
I will make into my room
to sleep in when it rains
because along
with every other reason
to get out of here
the ceiling in my real room
leaks

It's *Utter* Dark

at the end
of the trail
where the trees are thick
and tall and close

and the sun gets stuck
in the branches
and ripped apart
and dies
before it hits my roof

utter is from a song
Jimmy's got to think is about
his life
because he plays it like a theme

> *She cut my heart*
> *She stole my breath*
> *I knew she'd be*
> *The utter death*
> *Of me . . .*

my father
is the only one

who lives with me
and he's so funny

    Get your butt downstairs!

and when I get there

    What are you staring at?

plus he can yell
as loud
as anything
at the end of the trail
and no one hears

    Don't stand there
    Like a slug, Slug!
    Open a freaking can of soup.
    Do that at least!

that's funny
right?

Jimmy and Me

are like two sticks
that came down in a storm

you see them on the ground
the morning after
not touching
just near each other

I mean two things
that happen
to be in the same place
at the same time

this green house
right now

but in a year
if I make it
I might get out of here
I'll be sixteen

I'll be . . .

I'll be . . .

I don't know what

Mostly Jimmy's Sad

and crying in his chest
about stuff he maybe had
once in the past

also he hurts bad
from his leg
and spine which
he busted up (he says)
when I was small

I think he
mostly doesn't see me
living there with him

like I'm some fly
that buzzes in
and buzzes out
while he's at home
and who he knows
will finally fly out
and stay out
like my mother did

that's not a joke
she really did

My Mother Left

just after I was born
a year
and a month or two

it's like she said

    Nine months for this?
    No thanks.

or maybe not

take this morning in the schoolyard
parking lot
the mothers (and one grandfather)
dropped their kids
then chatted loud like a television scene
of normal life

but that's not us
Jimmy and me

he says she died
my mother died
but he doesn't tell me how

and talks instead
about Utah
or Idaho or Colorado or
one of those states
out there
he says she was from

Jimmy never says
the same state twice
if he talks about her
(which isn't much)

but I look up
each place anyway

Rusty Gold

you wouldn't think ten
miles from here is a twenty-
million-dollar house
but there are lots of those

they call this part
of my state the gold coast
with huge rich
houses on the beach

but here stuck off
the trail that time forgot
there's only tin

and with a little creek
at the bottom of the slope
tin goes brown and flakes to rust
real fast
like that old pickup
semi-rotting in the yard
so we have rust stuck
smack in the middle of the gold

ha Rusty Gold

sounds like the kind of
country star my father listens to

My quivering heart
    Beats just for you . . .

then turns it up
and drinks and sleeps
or drinks and cries
into his hands

I'd call myself that

hi, I'm Rusty Gold

except it wouldn't
stick

not stick
like

Slug.

or like the other name they
love to call me

It Was the Fourth

day of school this year
the hallway after seventh period
I'd almost cleared
my first week without saying much
or being seen

when

a kid a junior his clothes
reeking of sour gym shorts
passed me quick
I felt him swing around
and stop and tug his friend back
half laughing eyes widening
as he'd found the answer
to something big

   It's him!

and some cold hand twisted my stomach
into a boiling wet towel

no, you don't see me
I didn't say

but the second kid half laughing now
let himself be dragged right
over to my face

    Really? Is it you?
    We were just talking about you.

I looked down the hall
to the doors too far away

    It's him. I know it is.

what?
I said
that's all just
what?

    You actually live there?
    The green house in the junkyard.
    Is that where you live?

    It is. I saw him once.
    What's your name?

I wanted to say *nobody*

and poke his eye out
but said nothing

I think his name is Junk.

said the second one

He lives there.
Let's call him it. Junk.

Hey, Junk,
How much for a
Twenty-oh-eight
Subaru fender?

the half laughing was all
laughing now

I Never Was

great to begin with
not a zippy
super gift of happy fun
from anyone to anyone

I am fifteen
can barely touch the top
of the doorframe
with my fingertips
if I jump for it

have puppet
strings for muscles
am not good
with bats and balls
and sticks and goals

my throat closes
and I choke
when Coach
makes me run in gym

the reason is
my lungs are flat

and small as
as
as
I don't know
tea bags

Plus

my face is kind
of narrow
like a wedge
from my nose
back to my ears
and my chin
comes to a point

Nine months for this?

maybe my mother said
or maybe not

but some kid said to his mom
once in a store
(because I have to shop
for food and soap)

He's scary.

and I am scary
especially in the dark
when only half
my ax-head is lit

and the other's not

you'd say so too
if you looked in
my mirror

But I See

even if I don't talk
I look at things
(and sometimes people)
what they look like
what they do

last week at lockdown assembly
there was a girl from
my middle school
in the row in front

I looked at her hair too long
didn't turn my eyes away
from that waterfall of hair
before she looked around and saw and
made a face that said

    Why do they even let freaks in our school?

sometimes I don't know
how long I do it
(stare from my eyes
at a thing or face)

at home Jimmy says

Don't stare at me.
God, you're like her.
She was always staring at me
Looking for answers.
I hate that.
I don't have any answers.
Does it look like I have answers?

so when I can
I keep my head down
and eyes down
and look away

still
I see things

The Teachers Stopped

asking Jimmy
to come in

And talk to us about Robert.

because he kept
missing meetings
and when they called
he'd say

I'll make it right.
I'll talk to him.

but he didn't make it right
or talk to me
and when they said

You know we thought
At first that he was slow.
But he's not slow.
Your son's not slow at all.
He's just quiet, very quiet.

he'd shrug and say

Yeah, I guess.

there was a time
a social worker came
but Dad found out
and cleaned the house
and made a meal

I played along
because I didn't know
what they would do
but I knew him
and it was easier

one time he almost choked
on what a counselor said
when she called

Join a club? A school club?
Him? Seriously?
Good luck with that.
I mean, I'll ask him, but . . .

and flicked a look at me
then rolled his eyes
across the ceiling between us

of course he never asked
about me joining any club

not even
ha
the human race

I was good enough
to live at the dark end
of a dark trail
but not much else

not that I was going to join
anything anyway
but still

he never talked to me
he never asked
I never joined

I Never Joined

but if I look along and up
the valley from my house
I can spy
the sharp white finger
of the church's tower
pointing away
from us

the church the church
why do I look up there?

because of her
my mother maybe
I don't know

it is the parish church
of St. Dominic
which dad says she
baptized me at

Father Percy
is the guy who runs it

when I went to church
he talked from his pulpit
low and slow
like he was making up
each word before he said it
but (surprise) it sat there
like the page
of a book
when he was done

yeah
I used to go to church

maybe it was knowing
my mother held me
at that baptism bowl
and maybe I liked
to think of my mother
still in my life

or maybe I went
because there was a girl
red hair and freckly
from another school
her hands pressed flat together
at the rail not looking at me

but
oh boy
that red hair

Father Percy Talked One Day

about guess what

God

and God's two other selves
there are a total of three of him
in heaven
taking shifts
to get it all done

but none of them
I think
get around to
the end of the trail

When There Is

no moon
the woods are blue
along the trail

the only light
the only real light
is tiny simple clean and bright
a yellow lamp
peering through the trees
far up the other way

it's from a shed
on the far side
of the churchyard

I Went Up There Once

a couple of years
ago to see
after all what the heck
was going on
this pinhole
of bright buttery light
blinking down my woods
at night

so I crept up the slope
and looked in
a little lighted shed
and there he was

Father Percy bent
white-haired and squinting
over a table
over a little book
over a page
his pointer finger
moving under a line
on the page

I thought he must be

making up
the speech
he gives on Sunday

thou shalt not
do this
or this
or this
or be this either

then all at once
I saw his face turn
to the window
so I ducked

but I guess
he only saw
the night-black square
of glass
not me

because when
I peeked again
he was back
at the line
on the page

in the book
on the table

so I went home
that night
and that was that

He Preached Another Time

from his altar how
soft eyes will see
the great big world
and let it in

but hard eyes are
armor iron-hard
against the world
a visor with no slit
that only keeps
the big world out

he said how you swim
around in life

and life (like water)
comes in through your sight
if your eyes are soft

but how you have
no openings
only yourself
inside you
if they're hard

Now can you guess, my friends,
What sort of eyes
Our Savior had?

the kids waggled their hands
their parents smiled
that girl nodded
her red-haired head
and said she had soft eyes too

See, Mommy?

then she blinked
just before she left
and moved away

sometimes I wonder
what kind of eyes
I have

maybe I have
one of each

Jimmy Listens

to songs about cowboys
who rot in jail
for robbing banks
and stealing cars (and hearts)
and shooting lovers dead
down by the river
or the railroad tracks

basically breaking
one by one
all Father Percy's
ten commandments

some of Jimmy's songs
are kind of funny

> *I busted up the town tonight*
> *Butt-drunk on gin and ale*
> *But just as I was taking flight*
> *They spied my butt*
> *And caught my butt*
> *And tossed my butt in jail!*

some are not so funny

some of his songs
just make you hurt inside

The preacher finally comes and calls,
I weep and tell my sin,
But these old moldering prison walls
Just keep on closing in.

which pretty much
is school
and every day
and every place
for me

At School You Learn

that maybe there's
a third kind of eye
the one that's sharp
and tries to dig inside you
to your private place
and call you out
and make you talk
so all the other eyes
can stare at you

it was yesterday
just after sliding in my chair
when Mr. Mark bubbled out my name

Bobby, what might the answer be?

how many eyes turned to me

Hmm? What's your best guess?

how many burned on me

Do you remember how we covered this?

I knew the answer
was stumbling too far back
in my brain
caught in the clawing branches
to bring out right away
so I shook my head

then in sixth period

Can you read this out for us, Bobby?

Miss Pagelli tossed this off
like the world was
a fun place

and the snickering
started when
like the old man in the shed
I dragged my finger
under every word

Yeah Teachers Sure

here and there
maybe one a year
or none some years
they look and frown

> *Bobby, do you want to talk?*
> *Bobby, is there a reason*
> *Your paper isn't done?*
> *Bobby, Bobby, Bobby?*

but I slip past and fall
between the lines
and off the page

I don't add up
I don't react the way
the lab instructions say

I fumble
don't connect
am left behind
aside off-center
and so far backstage
I'm in the parking lot

and they don't follow me
teachers don't
they can't
how can they follow me
unless I leave a trail
for them
unless I help

Help us help you.

but I don't

because we know
both you and me
you and me together know

one less like me is good
one less is easier
one less is fine
one less of me is more
for all the rest

So After School

I shut my mouth and
keep it shut

and hours go by
when I don't speak a word

at the end of days
like that
my voice
is scratchy
from not speaking

I've kept it
for myself
to use or not

those are good days

A Thousand Million

things that
jam my head
and burn my eyes in every class
fly off when I set foot
inside
the wood

that noisy acid
rain they pour

> *It's him again.*
> *Who?*
> *Junk.*
> *What's his problem?*
> *Problemssss. Plural.*
> *Where'd he get that head?*
> *Watch what he does.*
> *Look. Look!*

until my
scalp and neck and shoulders
ache so hot
and my eyes go blind

but the quiet in the woods
the quiet of the woods
the quiet washes all of it away
and the air *quivers*
like wings humming

and all that humming
hums around you
and inside you
if you let it
through the eight or nine
holes in the human body
not counting pores
but including eyes

I take the rough path
from the street
and step up
on the flat packed
dirt of the trail
and like the myth guy
when he touches ground
I start to pull myself
into myself
and make myself
again

Every Day I Stop

two point three miles from my house
where the trail narrows
between ledges of rock
where the road for the rails
(the rail road)
was blasted flat
out of the slope

there is a bare foundation
just after this narrowing
a footing
of stone brick concrete
where a long gone
rail shed stood
or utility station

every day I stop
go to the edge and look down

the slope
is steep
some eighty feet
to the rocky creek
below

a scary sight if you were
a railroad passenger

it scares me too but
every day I stop
step to the edge
look down
at the moving creek

and wish

I were

two point three million miles from home

It Was Dinnertime

or should have been
when I jumped inside
from those busted steps
but

instead of putting supper
on the table
for me
(his only son)

instead of dishing
out hot food

   Come and get it, Bobby!

dad pulled a deck of cards
from a drawer
kicked out a chair
and plunked down
at the kitchen table
with two open beers
(he was alone)

frying myself an egg

I said

this is a junkyard
a dump
of junk

he looks up at me
like he's not sure
who I am

    Didn't you have an egg this morning?

I didn't bother
to say
it's all there was

    That many eggs a day will kill you.

they all know this place at school
crap all over the place
they call it a junkyard—

Jimmy gestured
with his hands as if
so what?
then said aloud

So what?
What do you want
Me to do about it?
You don't like it?
Clean it up.

me? it's your garbage
it breaks you kick it
off the deck
you should get rid of trash
like normal people do

You live here.
Besides, shut your mouth,
I work.

doing what?
picking up your disability check?

Shut your mouth.
I do jobs.
When I can.
The government is tough.
You can't work too much.
Besides . . .

he dealt four hands
of five cards each

 . . . what do you care
 What morons say?
 But, hey, Slug, if you don't like it,
 You can clean it up.
 In fact, if you don't clean the yard . . .
 If you don't . . .

what?
if I don't clean it
what?

 I'll think of something worse.
 Do it this weekend
 Or else.

I can't do it all myself

 Yeah, well, he said, *I won't do any of it.*

I thought of the camper
my mother's camper
on cinder blocks

in the
corner of the yard
my secret plan

can we
at least get a big
trash container?

    Can I win the lottery?

which Jimmy thought was funny
and laughed at
as he hovered
over the cards of three
imaginary friends and
turned some over

he kept laughing
even after
I left the room
with a curse in my head
a straight finger in my pocket
and thinking

well, that didn't go well

On the Other Hand

one good thing
about an impossible task
is that it's impossible

and because it's impossible
it becomes real simple

it's like

    Hey, fix the world by three o'clock or else!

which you could never do
so any little thing you try
seems like

    Well, it's a start.

so after school the next day
I dumped my pack
on my still unmade
(always unmade) bed
and went out back

what a gross hole

a total mess
of
of
of
rubbish litter trash scraps
and God knows what all
but I pretended
a twenty-foot container
was standing empty over there
and tugged on gloves
and started hauling
crap to where it wasn't

the coffee table first
which when I lifted
by its legs
like a dead goat
a herd of chipmunks
living under it
scattered away

clocks radios bent pipes
two sinks with busted faucets
chairs and rags
and lamps and random
lumber shingles window frames

to have some fun
I rolled five bald tires across the yard
like that hoop game
and raced two tires at once
that flopped over when
they hit the pile

pretty soon I had a mound
of trash
like a bonfire ready to burn
and saw patches of bare ground
I never had

I kept on it
wrenching dragging heaving tossing
all the reject wasted rubbish
I could move

until it was too dark
and I was tripping over stuff
and anyway my arms and back
throbbed from the strain
and said

   No more.

so I stopped for the night
and leaning on
the kitchen door
to breathe and look around
I found that after
three and a half hours
phase one
of doing
the impossible
was done

well
(I thought)
it's a start

it was a start
all right
I didn't know it then
but just after
I started cleaning
up the mess
but just before
the next day passed
the real mess
had begun

I Never Take

the bus

I'd rather crawl
on naked knees
across a field of dented beer cans
or swim a lake of pus

Jimmy cared
as much as flies
about what I did
and where I was

so no
no bus
ever

which was why
the next day
as I waited
and wandered
like I sometimes do
until the bells were done
and started down
the empty halls

toward the front

I saw a thing happen

The Art Room Door

was wide open
when I passed
and there was sudden noise
an angry voice
growling and spitting
in there

looking in I saw
two girls and a woman
not a teacher

the woman was leaning over
a skinny girl
with curly brown hair
while the other girl
stood shaking at a table
in the corner
her hands
on her face
her face pale
as paper

Ever! Ever! Ever!

was the only word
I heard clearly

the woman said it
through her teeth
then slapped
slapped
slapped
the skinny girl on her face
like she would slap a man

it was the opposite
of a sweaty schoolyard fight
this was cold and sharp as icicles

that cold froze up my chest
while the woman spun
past me
her shoes clacking fast
and angry down the hall

I shrank to nothing
watching
the skinny girl go
shaking shaking
to the other one

and hug her
kiss her wet face
and her lips

oh okay

but the other one
pried herself loose
twisting her shoulders back
and brushed by me
down the hall
the other way

uh . . .

I started to say but
shut straight up when
the skinny girl
wheeled around to me

> *What are you staring at?*

nothing

> *So?*

Help me.

help you?
do what?

Take them! Hang them up!
The show's next week!

this skinny girl
had dark short hair
in a mess of curls
a frayed T-shirt
almost off one shoulder
and faded jeans
and a sort of face
hard not to look at
and her cheek raw red

are you okay?

but she only looked away
scooping up a pile of big paper
art paper
pictures
in her arms
from the corner table

Get the rest. Come on.

get the rest come on

I wanted to ask
what that was all about
the shouting and the slapping
(I got the kissing part)
but already she was
somewhere else in her mind

I Started Taping Art

up on the wall
with her
in the hall
outside the art room

    Not there. There. No. There.

when Mr. Taymore
the art teacher
rumpled down the hall
and came to look
bending here and there
to study close
then standing back
to see it whole

    Good. Good. Rachel, are you
    Supervising your friend?

she (Rachel)
looked at him
then at me

    Yeah. But I've never seen him.

I don't know who he is.

I . . . I . . .

but what came out
was just a whisper
so the teacher
stood back again and frowned

   Well, it's looking good. Keep going.

he went away
she gave me a grin
of teeth with no smile in it
and I kept on taping

I had joined a thing
I guess
but don't remember
really choosing to

After a While

still in a whisper voice
I asked

are these good
the pictures?
good art?
I mean
I don't know

she stopped and looked
at me as if *duh*
then
cupped
her hand on her mouth
and heaved a pretend puke
into her palm

I knew that move
and hated it
felt stupid and went cold
with sweat completely
through my shirt
but snorted an almost laugh
at it anyway

then she unzipped this
big black flat case
and took out a board
with a sheet of tissue paper
on a drawing underneath

she peeled the tape
off the tissue corners
she did it slow

> *This, if you want to know,*
> *Is good. This is mine.*

and on the paper was
a bowl of fruit
lit by a candle on
the old table
in the corner
of the art room

from gray chalk on creamy paper
she had made
two ripe apples
(one with a thumbprint
of a bruise)

three pears two bananas
a bunch of grapes
that had been rinsed
and heaped in the bowl
which looked (the bowl)
light blue but
like every other thing
was only gray

and a peach
a single peach sat on the table
next to the bowl
looking yellow
red
and in between
the colors fiery
like it was perfectly
ripe

I knew the lines that made
every one of those fruits
were flat
as flat as the sheet
the lines were on

but all the fruit was

wet under the candlelight
as if it had been rinsed
just now
and just now
being served
to us
and real
enough to eat

but most of all what
sat there on the table
that peach drawn
with gray chalk
and only chalk
punched me in the chest

That Peach

was sitting there
on the surface of the table
except not sitting
it was touching lightly
on the wood

and the seam
between each half
was just a little blurred
and looking
like the peach might roll
right off the paper

I Hate to Talk

hate hate hate
to talk
dumb words
but standing there
in front of that light blue
bowl of wet fruit
pinned flat to the wall
and the blurring
fiery peach

I almost reached to catch
the thing
before it rolled
off the table
to the floor and at my feet
and found my tongue
and the breath from my lungs
pushing into sound

hey
I don't get how
you can do that
how you can see that way
the shapes

and more than shapes
the
the
weight things have
with just lines
flat lines and circles and edges
and make them seem
to move
how do you see
that way?

which is more words
than I have said
since second grade
so I stopped and thought she
might take over now
and maybe say

    Wow, Bobby, thanks!

but when
she turned to me
rubbing her cheek wet open raw
like her skin was turned inside out
she shook and
sank down the wall to the floor

that lady

I started to say but
didn't know where to go with that plus
I felt as visible as
I don't know
a giant turd
on a clean white rug
but my mouth went on

that lady is
your
mother?

she pulled up her shirt
to wipe her face her cheeks

    I hate her.
    She's such a—

and used a word
not from a country song

well, why did she—

What's not to get?
You already saw why.

which I guess I did
this girl and
that girl
and this girl's mother saw them

she shouldn't do that

No, really?

she coughed into her shirt
still shaking

She knows. She'd be stupid not to know.
I mean, come on.
She has no idea about anything.
I had to keep her from hitting
Maggi.
She's out of her mind. God,
I hate my life.

she said *hate* like the snap of a whip
then breathed and breathed
so hard

I almost felt the heat
and my tongue moved again

my dad's a jerk

which was so random
that I stopped while she clamped
her eyes tight shut
and let some tears squeeze out

> *My father's moving out.*
> *Soon.*
> *She thinks he won't,*
> *But he will, and I'm going.*
> *She can't keep me anymore.*

All this is way too much
to know
I thought about that
beat-up camper bus
and how right now
I wanted to be in it

> *She should just . . . die.*

another word that cut a hole in the air

Fall off a cliff or something.

what the hell?

she growled in her
throat like a tiger
and her paste-white face
(pasty except for one red cheek)
went all pink

I don't even know.

her eyes
didn't stay put
in one place
her head kept moving
the whole time
she talked

She's always on me—
"Don't you dare, don't you dare."
And church. She wants me
To go to church all the time.
God, I hate that place.

I was almost going to say
I see the church from my house
and soon would spy it from
the windows
of a camper junked
in my yard
and spy
on the world
through the thick trees
to the churchyard
and beyond
but suddenly that was weird
and I made myself
not say it

waiting I guess
for me to talk
which I did not
she finally taped her
picture to the wall said

    Thanks for whatever.

and walked away
grumbling and growling
to or at her mother

or herself
or maybe me

which I did too
only silently
in my head

There Was a Girl Once

I gave a ring to
when I was seven
it was second grade
near Christmas

a ring I found
on the bathroom
floor at home

it looked like
one of Mom's old ones
dad must have
gotten mad
and thrown

it must have rolled behind
the sink
(I thought)
and he forgot

it was silver
it didn't have a jewel but
it gleamed when I buffed it

(then I didn't know
now I would)

I didn't tell him
I took the ring to school

Wow, Bobby, thanks.

this girl said
when I gave it to her

the words I might have said
when I gave her the ring
didn't come
but I hoped
she knew it meant
I liked her

God knows where
I got the idea
of rings
tv and movies and songs
about other kinds of people

(now I'd know)

later her friends came
up to me
three or four of them

    She told us about the ring
    You gave her.

yeah?

    Is it . . .

(is it meant to say I like her? yeah)

    Is it, is it . . .
    Is it the ring from a bathtub plug?

from . . . what?

    The rubber plug from a bathtub drain.
    The ring you pull.
    It looks like that.

what? no
but they laughed

    Here. She says thanks—

one said
handing it back

but another said

    She didn't say that.
    She said, Bobby Lang?
    And then did this.

and did a fake puke
motion in the
cup of her palm

so yeah
I don't talk to people now
I don't do anything
but walk to school
and walk back home

except when I forget
and say something
anyway

and I said something
that afternoon

outside the art room door

I said so little
but I think it was
too much

Which Is All Fine

I'm pretty much
a thing nobody cares
about except to mock
(here's Rusty Gold again)

> *They call him "Junk."*
> *And sometimes "Slug."*
> *He ain't no hunk.*
> *The girls say, "Ugh!"*

but the question is
one question is
who's this sudden girl
with tangled brown hair
a frayed red shirt
nearly off her shoulder
and faded jeans
who hijacked me
who tugged me in

who doesn't like her mother
hates her in fact
and God and church
all stuff I didn't need

or want to know
and
and
she likes a girl
I know I know
she likes a girl
but still

Still what?

I don't know

That's right, you don't.

it was dumb
just dumb
so dumb

I had to get out
of there
and far away

the halls blurred past
and bright cold air washed
over me when I pushed
through the doors

and out across the lot
and toward the trail

girls

who cares

who cares

except

Except There's Always

a girl
even from when I was small
a thing about a girl
some girl
any girl
red hair no hair
I don't know

it's everywhere
tv school dads internet comics songs

Which girl
Of all the girls
Is the one true girl
For me?

you're supposed to
the whole world tells you to
you gotta find
some girl
some girl
some girl
or you won't be normal

you won't be right
or regular
you won't be correct

okay I get it
but they're probably not
and really can't be
thinking

of

her

One Hundred and Twelve Minutes

after that
bizarro scene
I'd chucked
my backpack
on my bed and
walked out back
chewing on what
in the world
all that crazy was
supposed to mean

then
took a breath
and emptied
my head

and busted up
a dozen crates
and splintery two-by-fours

then pounded out
their nails on a stump
(nicked my knuckles

and put a neat hole
in the top
of my left thumb)

then stacked the lumber
under the deck
against the house

all this
took me till late

(a time lapse
would be cool
to look at)

it was eight by then
I shut off the flashlight
and sat on the stump
until the dark and quiet
were all there was

I breathed
the night in
wanted to climb up and
walk slow along
the trail to calm myself

but had to bandage
my thumb hole

I stood
brushed myself off
and scanned one final time
through the trees

to spot that wink of yellow
half a mile up the valley

and wondered
with no answer at all
what the thing really was
with this girl

when I turned
to go inside I saw
a hundred yards
beyond my house
exactly opposite the church
another light

a fine fiery dot
of orange
sprinkled with black

the burning ash
of a cigarette lifted
to a mouth
glowing bright
then dulling

bright then dull

a cigarette in the woods

as much as my father
smokes (and that's a lot)
he never would
not on the trail
and hated finding butts
in the woods

They'll kill us all.
The hopeless morons.
Firestarters.

the ash glowed lamplight bright again

Hey! It's late.

it was my dad leaning off
the deck

watching me look
beyond our roof

    Get in here.
    I'm locking up.

by then
the orange light
in the woods above
from someone else
had winked itself out

Friday Came

crawling through
the window on my face

the ceiling sagged
but no more than
last night so
that was good

same face in the mirror
different shirt though
(no way could I wear again
what I'd sweated
through last night)

had an orange juice
an egg and toast
in a weak triangle
of hazy light
on the tabletop

out of the house
and on the trail
before my father woke (the usual)

something was different
a frost last night
the leaves the light
a sharpness up my nose behind
my eyes

an oak leaf
fell from unseeable branches
slowly slow

I counted seconds
then lost count
watching the leaf
dip turn float *sway*
but started again
it was
a minute nearly

even though its fall
was no fall because it sometimes
floated sideways or even up
like it didn't care
like it was having fun
before it touched the packed dirt
of the trail bed

I watched it settle there
dizzy from its fall
watched it settle in
watched it sleep

until the crows

those jet-black jokers
laughed their ugly laughs
in the black branched trees
like a gang of bullies
knowing stuff
you never could

cackling there
like witches over a curse

and thanks a lot it all comes back
my throat goes tight
and I remember now

I'm on my way
to
school

I Didn't Want to Think

about the art room slap girl
who kisses girls
just tried to make
hard eyes at everything

but they (my eyes) said

Ha. You wish.

and started spotting her
and only her
in the halls
in the caf
in classrooms that I passed

my head was down
was always down
but all at once my
eyes go

Look!

and there's her face
like a full moon in a black sky

a fiery peach
on a field of gray

by third period I couldn't not
look for her
and always found her

why?

who the heck is
Rachel Braly
anyway?
(I saw her name
on her art)

I want to say get out
my brain's too cramped
and full of junk
I have my stuff
leave me alone

>   *Hey, she's not looking for you, Junk.*
>   *You're looking for her.*

you don't know what
you're talking about—

but boom
just before
the day clamped shut
and I could run home free
there she was again

Final Period

I stood next to last
in the gym line
with that rock-brained pig
(I don't need
to say his name
everyone knows him)
standing behind me

    Hey, Junk, feel that?

I turned

feel what?

he thudded my arm
with a fist of brick

    That.

which started the
pummeling
punch after punch
in the same place

And that. Also that.

until he saw Coach
look stupidly up
from his stupid clipboard

I never guessed
the sick-gut
feeling you can get
from being punched hard
anywhere

maybe he shook
loose the last gob
of acid from my throat
and it splashed into
the sick pool of my gut

whatever it was
vomit sudden and hot
coughed up my throat
into my mouth
I doubled over
saw the door across
the gym to the lot outside
and staggered to it

Coach from his clipboard
shouted

>Hey, Lang, what the heck?
>Get back—

then through the door
three steps four five
before that burning bile
lurched up and out
and on the yard
a swamp of thin white goop
on the ground
behind the b-ball hoop

it came and came
then came the sting
of smoke
burning my sick-filled
burning nostrils

I looked up

and it was her

Her

I hate hate hate
this part of my brain
I'm in right now
if it's the part
all this junk
is clunking around in
but there she is

her bright eyes looking
like she knows she's smart
and something about
her hair the way
how even though it's short
it curls all over

I know I know
she's got a girlfriend
that's so not it

   Isn't it?

she can draw
a peach that moves

a peach so real
that real peaches
can look at it
and understand
what
being a peach
is
all about

but she never smiles
not real smiles
not when I look at her
just these flat stretches
of her lips
a kind of cold slit
and anyway her
freezing smiles
don't make it to her eyes
which like I said are bright
but seem just now as if they're
reading a bad word

what makes her not
like any of the others?

I know I shouldn't ask

I know I know
but I don't know

still there she is
behind the trash bin
squinting at me
her fingers stained with paint
pulling a smoking cigarette
out of her mouth
slowly like she knew I was
no threat

I spat out the last
of the slop

    You should do it in your hand.

she said

    Puke in your hand.
    It's funnier.

Again That Thing

came back to me and I
didn't want to go there
so I said

somebody was smoking
on the trail last night

which was like
nothing to her

    They don't really call you Jerk?

I spat out the last spit

Junk

I said
stupidly

they call me Junk

she stepped toward where
I was getting up

Because of where you live?

how did she know

it was you on the trail

I had to get out.

at first I didn't
say anything

My father finally gave up and left.
I told you, right? Well, he moved out last night.
It's just me and her now.
God, just looking at each other is like
A storm of razor blades.

I saw that storm
slivers of silver
slicing
across the breakfast plates

Everything she thinks hurts.
Mothers are the worst.

I wouldn't know

I didn't say

I couldn't tell if
she was
in the middle
of a conversation
with herself
or wanted to talk
to me and only me

(maybe because of what I saw
in the art room
and what I said
about her peach)

but she stopped then
took another drag
there was no noise
so I said

I'm the opposite

    What?

it's just me and my father
Jimmy, I mean

he's . . . yeah . . .
kind of a jerk too

I had no idea where
my words were
coming from

    Does he drink?
    My father does, a little.

mine too
not a little though

    Everybody does
    Except my mother.

and her face again
was all I could look at
I couldn't
not look at it
not see it
like money
on the sidewalk
your eyes go
right to

I know I know
she'll probably yell

    Stop staring!

but she didn't
like she had hard eyes
seeing only what's inside

    Maggi.

I looked around

where?

there was no one
there but us

    My mother in the art room.
    She's so clueless, but I guess
    That was the first time she actually saw us.
    So that's why
    All you saw . . .

okay
I mean, I get it

you and Maggi
is she okay
after that
I mean you're both still . . .

I had no clue
where I was going

    Yeah. She was freaked, but mostly, yeah.

okay yeah

    But now my mother
    Wants the priest,
    Can you believe it,
    To reformat me
    Or something.

Father Percy?
I said
then said
for how long?

    I don't know, however long an exorcism
    Takes. Or whatever. It's not going to happen.

no, I mean
Maggi
how long have you . . .

    A few weeks. God,
    Do you ever blink?

I tore my eyes off her
and looked away

    Freaky.

she said then stubbed
her cigarette
under her shoe

    By the way,
    You have a big gob of puke
    On your sleeve.

thanks

    Hey, if a friend doesn't tell you,
    Who will?

friend?

at the same time
that she turned away
Coach pushed out the door

Lang, what the heck?
You okay?

uh

Because if you're done
Throwing up,
You got two minutes
To change and get
To homeroom.

So That Day

was a stupid kind of joke

a punched-up arm
a puked-up shirt
sweaty underwear
the smell of vomit
in my nose
and her

    Friend.

her

    Freaky.

I ran off at the first
ring of the last
bell
kept my eyes hard and down
visor closed
didn't see her again
didn't see
anyone

good

The First Thing

after I got home
I walked right past
the growing mound of junk
as if I had a hoodie on
or blinkers like a horse

past all the other rubble
straight to the bus
her camper bus
that stood
just beyond the cleared
space I had made
to where the trees grew thick
and where the slope
continued sloping
to the creek

I wondered why and how
my dad (if it was him who)
drove the bus back there
and let it die
among the trees
so far from any road

why did he leave it there
and let the woods
grow into it?

was that the angry work
that mangled up his leg?

or did my mother drive
it to the back
and leave it there
before she bolted off
and died?

nah that's too sad
I almost laugh
at the crybaby story
I'm making in my mind
like a song by Rusty Gold

My mama left
   When I was born,
      She died without a fuss.
Now all I have
   To call my own
      Is her old camper bus.

right
the camper

the camper is the thing

the camper

the 1967 V-dub camper

It Was Cold Among the Trees

when I walked around
the hunk of dead metal
to see what was what

one headlight smashed apart
its eye-cup cupping rusty
water in its bowl
the other gone an empty socket

windshield covered over with a tarp
front bumper
twisted in the leaves
a dent deep up the nose
like a tree fell on it
tires gone wheels flaky brown
the whole thing up on blocks
without any tires
but otherwise
intact

I sniffed in at
the side door crack
at the moldering guts
a dozen years of rot

had left inside
then slid my fingers
in and wrenched
the side doors open

the damp
of how many
thousand days
and nights
had made
a home inside
the bus
for all of nature

a sea of crushed
and gutted acorns
the remains of
a million meals

the bathroom
for whatever
ate them
was there too
a mound
of poop the size
of walnuts

from I don't
know what kind
of furry animal

I shooed a pair
of mourning doves
out of the ceiling space
(mourning what?
no mother being here?)

and when I did
found little silver stars
of no real constellation
painted up there

the gone front windshield
was replaced inside by plastic sheets
taped hard in place
and good enough to stay

the rear window was
rusted shut
but that was some security

the curtains were
knotted and rotten

and the wood that made
the table and bed
was a kind of
slimy pressboard
gone bad in the rain

it folded like paper
so I tore it out
and dragged it to the heap

after a tough three hours
and the downing of the sun
I had nicked knuckles
scraped wrists and arms
plus an empty
shell of a camper van
that needed to be scoured clean

a worn-down broom
proved to be best
its bristles short and hard

I used it to brush
and scrape
the cobwebs from
the inside walls

then sweep
the dust straight out
which some of it
blew back on me

idiot
that I am I didn't think
to wrap a towel
on my face until
an hour into it

who knows what kind of
acid poison was already
eating my tea bag lungs

the doors were uneven
and wouldn't close
because of a deep dent
which no hammering
could undent

but I dragged a length
of wire from the heap
and made a loop
to loop around one door
and tied it to the other

and wound it tight
into a knot
so the doors nearly closed
then padlocked them
and knotted some wire
outside so I could use
the lock there too

it was decent enough
to keep the lions
and tigers and bears out
while I was in there
and everyone else out
when I wasn't

by flashlight
I razor-scraped the scum
off the side windows
and buffed them
with spritzer and the towel
from my face

then laid a plastic tarp
on the floor and duct-taped
it to the walls
as high as it could go

and hoisted down
my box spring
and a slew of pillows
from my room
and found a lamp
in the yard
and ran a cord
of cords out from the house
to plug it in
and there was light

then I had to tumble
the big trash heap over
to get at the coffee table
that was under it
which I needed for
a kind of nightstand

I took a leg for it from
a backless kitchen chair
and washed it all and sanded it
by hand
and set the table next
to the pillow end
of the bed

I was building
I was building
I realized when
I was nearly done
I was building
a fallout shelter

the opposite
of the open woods
a six-walled closed-up
space for me
and just for
me

lying there
and looking up
at the ceiling stars
I felt a tingle
of something far away
and gone

and realized that no
single part of me
did not hurt
or slightly bleed

I was spent
of nearly
everything

and only realized then
that I'd been
out there
all night long

so long
in fact it must
be near
morning

I looked up
through the ceiling
of branches
at the still-black sky
and wondered what
time it was

when

just as I breathed in

I heard them

Church Bells

Prime hour
first hour of daylight
dawn
new morning
sunrise
day

(Father Percy talked
about the hour-bells
and called the first
one Prime—
which always rings at six
no matter
the time of year)

I stood there
tightening myself
fast and quiet while
the morning
daytime sunrise
bell rang
and rang

except

6 a.m.
in October
is still dark

still

night

black as
the inside
of a closed
and buried
coffin

(or a six-walled
metal room without
the lamp turned on)

one second all you are is silent
and the night
breathes low
like it's asleep

and dark
is like

a voice that could
but doesn't speak
(the best kind)

then

thunder
shakes the air
wide open
with an iron
hammer

clang
and
clong

quivering the wood
from one end
to the other
and quiet flies away

I stood there
leaning on the camper doors
the handle sideways in
my shoulder blade
and watched

for the light
to flutter down to ground

watched and watched

for morning

a new day

yes

except that no light came

what came was
something else

What the Hell Are You Doing?

my father from the house

What are you doing out there?

his voice a mad scribble
like a black crayon
in a two-year-old's
wrong hand
over the soft
humming
of the last bell

It's six a.m. You nuts?

I'm cleaning up like
you told me to

Who told you?

you said
get rid
of all this junk
you said I had to

No I didn't.
And I sure didn't tell you
To mess with that camper.
Get in here.

I latched the camper doors
and padlocked them
to keep him out
so he wouldn't pry to see
what I was making
what I had made in there

but he'd already
gone back inside

the jerk didn't remember
his big *or else*
so now I have black lung
and bloody fingers
and animal poop poison
eating my veins

but at least my own
new room

my own new room
at last

He Was at the Table

again already where
he usually is
his bad leg jutting
straight out from the
chair and table legs

I can't walk. It's bad today.

I looked at him
his head waggled
on his neck

uh-huh

I need you to pick up a package.
He's waiting for you.

this early?

he said nothing

you mean, Mike?

No, come on. It's Ray.
It's Ray on Saturdays.

then Jimmy gave me a five

If he calls to tell me
You didn't show . . .
You understand?

I've done it before

If you steal my money,
You won't even know
How fast your head will spin.
You understand?

got it

And get right back.
I'm timing you.

I took the five
and climbed the valley
to the road

twenty minutes street to street
to find his friend waiting
inside his open garage

as if he
sold weapons not beer

he said nothing
just took the five
and gave me a paper bag
heavy with a six-pack
while his wife or someone
in a bathrobe
stared gray-faced
from the front window

I Passed the Church

on the long way home
(I wanted Jimmy's beer
to be as warm as possible)

Father Percy
was outside
the arched red door

(*no, Father, this isn't*
an offering
for the food campaign)

a woman was crying
sobbing really
both to and at
the priest
tugging his sleeve
and saying

    She she she!

and it was her

the mother from the school

Rachel's mother
the one who slapped her hard
and ran away

the one who hates
what Rachel is and does

and he was listening hard
head bent to her
(the way he bends it
when he reads)
nodding very slow
his hands on one of hers
saying what back
I didn't hear

I noticed just now
how thin
the woman was
(where Rachel gets it from)
except with hair pulled
wire-tight and stiff
and limbs
all wound up like a coil
ready to unspring

this slapping woman
shook on her heels as if
she might fall over
or fly off

her screaming whisper
in his ear
was just that word

   She!

the car keys in her
other hand
kept jangling
with each

   She she she!

meaning

   Bad bad bad!

her gasps and tears
between her teeth
were angry mad

I remembered
Rachel saying

. . . she's out of her mind . . .

Father Percy took
one of his hands
and set it
on her shoulder now
turning to the door

Come in, come in.

and led her through
the arched red door
into the lobby
of the church

but something of
that woman
remained outside with me

a kind of cold
in the air
like frost
and eyes that speared me

with their pointed tips
as if I'd done
a bad thing
was unclean
had lied
had stolen
something precious
from her
and she knew it
and would get me
for it
she would get me back

I shivered
then remembered dad

by then the bag
was soaked
and I walked home

where he shouted tilting
from the tilted deck
why would I ever *ever* take
the long way back
and now his beer was ruined

(and in my mind
I smiled
and in my pocket
my middle
finger
went stiff again)

Wednesday

the weather changed
and cold came in for real
closing up the world
with clouds
that wouldn't budge

gray sky
gray air
gray ground
all gray
like everything
was drawn in gray

I hadn't spotted Rachel
since last week
and wondered
was she sick
or mad at me
(because I'm so important)

or did something
happen with her shouting mother
something I wanted not
to want to know

when all at once
there she was
standing still
looking at me
in the art room hall
with all the pictures
finally up

I didn't know what my face
did but I took a step
then stopped

her eyes were dark like
inside glass at night
no depth in them
the surface of a frozen pond
cold slipped up my arms
across my shoulders fingering my neck

uh, Rachel?

then
like her inside eyelids blinked
and something fell away
there I was
in front of her

Guess what?

she said

Can you help me?
Nobody can help me.

friend?
help?

who am I
to
her?

then she cupped her hand
her same puke hand
beside her mouth
and bent close to my ear
her breath on my neck
like whispering a secret

To see an art high school
I might transfer to.
I sent some art and wrote
The best essay.

something went tingly
when she was this close
and told me this

as if it was a move
the opposite of puking
in your palm

as if I knew a secret now
that no one knew
but me

that's cool

I said

except
why should I be happy
she might leave our school?

> *Mr. Taymore got a friend*
> *Of his, a painter, to write a letter too.*
> *The school is in the city. It's really good.*
> *I'll live with my dad,*
> *Go to art school,*

And never see my mother again.
Win, win, win.

that didn't sound
much like a win at all
at least for me
and wasn't any secret

okay . . .

then she said

Come with me.
I don't want to go alone.
I mean, I can but I don't want to.

come?
with?
you?

All my other friends are artists.
They'd be jealous.
You wouldn't be. Right? You wouldn't?
My mother won't take me.
We can get an Uber
To the station or

Your dad can drop us off.

oh
she needs me
for a ride

Yeah, come with me.
My dad'll buy us lunch.

she said over
her shoulder
as she walked away

The School Assembly

was Friday morning
I sat in a row
far from the goons
who call me Junk
it doesn't matter where

there were awards
it doesn't matter what for

someone
played the flute
I think and
someone
read a poem
two girls sang
it doesn't matter who

I heard Maggi laugh
from the fourth or fifth row
but not with Rachel
which I guessed I wondered why

then they said her name

Rachel Braly!

she won
the art competition
of course she did

and came up from some seat
I didn't see

her mother was there
in the audience
sitting alone
some kind of frosty
space around her

then utter weirdness
took over
when Rachel said

    Thank you for this prize.
    I owe it all to—

squinting her eyes to slits
she searched the seats
and pointed to her mother there
and said

My father.
Who couldn't be here today.

there came
a sudden hollow
in the room
a loud no-noise
in the air
and she grinned
and walked offstage

her smile was
was like
a cut
across her face
that didn't seem to hurt
her
only other people
or maybe only
her mother
who walked
up the aisle to the back and
out of the giant quiet room
her face
like a stone

I Thought Okay

this has entered some other
universe
I don't want to be in
don't need the buzzing in my ribs
my veins
my eyes

and maybe she'll forget
she said

    Come with me.

almost hoped
she would

but no

    Tuesday is great.

it had to be a weekday so

    Tuesday, okay?

and yeah

I said I'd go
don't ask
just don't

Jimmy Didn't Care

could barely limp himself
to the pickup
except that Rachel
was a girl
a breathing girl
and that was good enough

> *Hey, it doesn't matter what*
> *She looks like,*
> *Just as long as she's a girl.*
> *I was worried.*
> *We all were.*

I didn't say
she's so not interested
but just him saying that
made me
want to puke

plus I had no idea
who *we* were
unless his beer friends
Ray and Mike

we puttered through
the streets and roads
to where
she was waiting
not in or at or near
her house but on
some random corner
she told me to come to

my father gave her
a once-over
then he shrugged
and she sat between us
in the front
her black art case
in the space behind
the seat

My dad will meet us at Grand Central.

was the only thing
I remember
anybody said

my father squinted
and blinked the

whole way to the station
thinking I bet
when we got out

    (*Not a girly girl.*
    That's for sure.)

he didn't crack his wallet
no surprise
so she paid
for both our tickets
with a credit card

Jimmy was gone
before the train came

Onboard She Told Me

to sit
across from her
in a facing seat they have
near the doors

she unzipped her case
took out a sketchpad and pencils
arced her lips up
in a quick muscle smile
that went right away
and bent low over her pad

I have a huge folder,
Well, my dad does,
Of my drawings I did
In like kindergarten.

the train already started to slow
for the next station

I thought about
making a comic book once

It's awful, my early stuff.

He likes it.

her face when she
hung hunched
over the sketchpad
was all pinched up

like someone whose
eyes were pressed to
a microscope
trying to understand
a not-understandable
strange new thing

the train stopped and started again

her nose wrinkled
she chewed her lips
sucked her teeth
fussed her shoulders
up and down
as if spiders crawled
on her
not getting it
not getting it

(how I must look
when I read in class)

until the big bright face
that came
when she understood
and her fingers
loosened on the pencil
and went slack
and she sat back

(which never happens
when I read in class)

that was when
a passing train flashed by my face
and I pulled back
twitching until it was gone

she laughed a tinny kind of laugh

    I can't believe you
    Live fifty miles
    From the capital of the world
    And you've never
    Been on a train.

I love trains

    Pictures of them maybe.

after a while I said

you don't really
want your mom
to be like
dead?

she didn't look up
from the pad

    She can't see anything
    In my drawing. Nothing.
    She's like a blank.
    A mean blank.

then she showed me
what she drew

My Face

the ax-blade look
of it
my hair slanted
up on one side
as if I hadn't combed it
(I hadn't combed it)
she got all that
all right
as perfect
as a photograph

but

but

I wasn't scary here
I was what maybe
I thought I might
look like
if I wasn't me

but this *was* me

me in the half-light

from the window
sunlight on one side
shade on the other

but not scary somehow
not normal maybe
but still like there's
something going on
inside me that isn't
slow or mute or bad

and that she saw
and drew this
inside thing
on the surface
of the paper

making me seem
like I was just about
to talk
to talk!

and while she did all this
the train car
jumped and bounced
and jostled on the rails

I wanted her to tell me
what she did
and what she saw in me

and if it meant
and if I meant
something to her

but all I found to say was

cool
thanks

which was (again)
like I said nothing
because she blurted out
of nowhere

> *My mother prays for me, you know.*
> *Every day. While I'm sitting there!*
> *Whatever she prays for,*
> *I'm sure it's nothing good.*

then she held
her pencil out

Here, you draw something.

me?
what?
no
I can't draw

    Sit next to me.
    Draw her.

I think I blinked
and moved from
my seat up close to her

not a girly girl
but a girl
whose everything
was different
from anything

two rows away
a woman sat
she was middle-aged
maybe what my mother
might be now

(my stupid mind
made me go there)

I started with her head

    No.

Rachel took my hand
in her hand
her skin was cold
but her fingers fit
right over mine
and she moved my hand
pressing the pencil
here and lifting there
turning the point
sometimes
almost sideways
on the paper

after some minutes
the woman who
was not my mother
was not only
in her seat
but on the paper

wow

I said

and she said

   Eh.

Her Father

was supposed to meet us
at the station
it was the hugest room
roaring with bodies

Rachel looked around
but didn't see him.

>   *He'll be in a suit.*

a suit?
I laughed
that narrows it

then he trotted up behind her
and she hugged him

he shook my hand
he was okay
a guy a man a dad
whose mind
was only half with us

we walked fast

a bunch of blocks
up and over
or maybe down
there was a park
I don't know
it was mostly noise

the art academy
was a high school
taking four floors
of an old brick building
with gray stones
on the corners
and a heavy block
of gray stone
over the entrance

we took a tour
a lady showed us
classrooms and galleries
and studios

all through the rooms
and halls the smell of paint
which Rachel said was

Linseed oil and turps.

it stung my nose
but it was sweet too

students not leaning
over books but
over tables
boards and easels
that had long thin legs
spread out
to trip you up
when you walked
between them

and no student
none of them
not one of them
was doing with a pencil
what Rachel'd done
on a bouncing train

what she'd done

for me

Lunch Was Quiet

but loud too
I smelled myself
under the arms
and leaned away

there were four
trim maple trees
in the garden
outside the window
the tops were red
the leaves ready to fall
I thought of gray chalk
and some country songs
and Rusty Gold
and twenty-million-dollar homes
and yards full of junk
and I felt sick in
my stomach because
what the hell am I here for?

I had to use the bathroom

I got up
from the table

I didn't know
if I should say why
I got up

I have to—

 Just don't get lost, Junk.

her father looked up
from his salad plate

  Junk?

she laughed

  Nickname.

I almost did get lost
all that tile
and silver and light

when I came back I stopped

her dad was leaning close
to her
and tapping his finger

on the tablecloth
not looking right at her
but saying something
that she shook
her head at

    You lied to me!

she said
her face was pink
and raw
her shoulders bunched
against weights falling

I started for the table
but she was up
pulling a corner
of the tablecloth with her
shaking that off
and coming at me

what?
I said

    We're going back.
    To the station.

Unless you want to stay
With my father
Except I don't think
He likes you.

what?

Is that all you can say?
What? What?
Come on!

she grabbed my arm
and pulled me from the room

It Was Five Blocks

before she said
a word
then they came

    Weekend classes!

sorry?

    He said I could do weekend classes.
    That he's worried about her
    If we both leave.
    I said he promised me,
    But now he's all about her.

I tried to make my brain
go fast

you mean your mother?
if you move here?

    As if she's my job or something.
    I can't live with her anymore!
    She thinks she's so important,
    But she's not.

then still mad
still burning in her mind
she hooked her arm
in mine her
fingers wrapping mine
why I didn't know
and once by accident half put
half didn't
her head on my shoulder
for half a block
and didn't pull away
as if as if

and I felt something
I can't say what but
I felt I should
say some words

I like the picture

> *If I can't go to that school,*
> *If I can't go,*
> *I'll die.*
> *I will.*

and she pulled herself
from me unzipped her case
and threw her drawing pad
into a trash bin
and walked on

what the hell?

I pulled it out and
carefully tore out
her drawing
of my face and slid it
in my jacket

from that point
on until the train
she said nothing at all

except
the sputtering
in her veins
made it a loud
nothing

Out of the Tangle

of cars waiting at our station
Maggi
came running

    Rache—Rache—

and scooped Rachel in her
arms

    Did you get in? Did you?
    I missed you.

and their lips met and closed
on each other
as if I wasn't there
as if no one was there

    Maggs—

Rachel said but
a sideways ax blade of a car horn
flung its way across the lot
and screamed
to a stop in front of us

her mother Rachel's mother
in a fit behind the wheel

and Maggi
her face turned gray

I can't—

she said and backed up

You can't?

Rachel said

You can't what?

then Maggi skittered off between the cars

and Rachel's mother bounded out
wound so tight
and yelling out
so loud
in the public parking lot
as if
half the town wasn't there

No, no, not her.
Not any of this.
Living with your father?
Going to that school?
I won't let you.
You're already turning into . . .

and Rachel was right
at it
as if she'd been planning for this
on the train ride home

What? I'm turning into what?

You can't be there alone.
You'll get yourself killed.

You don't know anything.

You think you'll still see her?

Shut up about Maggi—

You little—

more and more

as if their words were
blood splatter
the noise they made
was like huge windows
shattering to
a million
jagged pieces
in my head

stop! I said *stop it!*

at which her mother
flung her flashing eyes
at me

> *How dare you come between*
> *My daughter and me?*
> *How dare you!*

Rachel started in among
the moving cars

my hands remembering
reached out
for her
a feeble move

all there was
was the breeze
of her not there

I know who you are!

her mother hissed
nailing me where I stood

And where you—

she gasped
the spit inside
her mouth

I know where you live.
Your father is a criminal, a jailbird.
Is that where you were born?
That garbage pit?

I stared at her
her hollow eyes
double black holes

Stay away from her!
Stay away, or I'll call the police!

but you
I didn't say
you
you're the one
you hit you smacked your daughter
she's fine if not for you
she's good if not for you
she's
she's

but the woman's eyes
had torn away
from me

she jumped into her car
which was still running

Friend Come with Me

I didn't know what
to do with all of that
except to find where Rachel was

I saw my father's truck
pulling into the lot
but I couldn't stop
no matter all the jangling
up and down
my bones

I caught up
two streets later

Rachel shook me off
just walked ahead
shouting to herself

it wasn't long before
her mother cruising
street to street found us

Get in the car!

I'm walking home—

      You little—get in the car now!

Rachel ran ahead
leaving me with
her screaming-mad mother

      And you!
      You'll end up in jail
      Like your father!

and more like that
until the car
screeched off again

I caught up
a second time
bleeding inside from what
her mother yelled at me

but I managed
somehow to say

Rachel it'll be okay
you won the prize

the school likes you
they want you there
you saw—

and stupidly
so stupidly
I reached I reached

thinking I guess
or no not thinking

I reached
I somehow could not
not reach for her

and slid my hand in hers
and held on tight like
on the streets before

when something snapped
she wrenched her hand away
and her blood-black eyes
ice-rimmed with red
shot back at me
and she fired this

What the hell?
Don't touch me, you freak!
I am not your girlfriend!

and then as if
both ends of a rope bridge
had been cut so I would fall

I fell

my mouth dropped open
and I stuttered

spluttered tongue-tied
I . . . I . . . I . . .

    Great comeback, Bobby.
    You know what?

but she was there again
her mother
beeping beeping

what Rachel said was lost
when she sprang away
and ran to the car

leaving me alone
on the street
with no stinking idea

what
just
happened

It All Exploded

in my head
when I got home
blind and stone-eyed

the bum was at his cards

I went there to pick you up—

I hate you!
I said
I hate you all!

Whoa, what the—

did you go to jail?
somebody said you went to jail
you never told me that
but it makes sense
you lie to me
you lie every second of the day
you probably lied to me about Mom too

Yeah, well, here's not a lie.
You're the reason your mother left.
You're the reason—

and suddenly my hands
were like knots
of wood on skinny stick arms
and somehow they
pulled back without me
doing it
and swung at him
one after the other

it was stupid to look at
like fighting a ghost
the first punch missed
a pathetic fly swat
but my right fist
got him square
on the jaw
my knuckles on the bone
and he slipped off
the chair and swore

and I watched
his bad leg buckle
the wrong way
to the floor

I Never Knew I Could

hit him
always the hurt of his
poor dumb old leg
stopped me

but now I knew
somehow I knew
his leg was part
of why my mother left
and maybe why she died
it had to be
so
I was hitting that
stupid leg
too

he lay helpless on the floor
and right away
(my hands were still
bunched up and ready)
I felt a hollow
in the center of my chest
unfisted my hands
and reached for him

Dad, I didn't mean to
I had a shitty day
let me

    No, you—

he swore a string of words at me
unrepeatable
even in my head
held up his shaking hand
to warn me off and slid
his bad leg awkwardly
across the floor between us

    Get away from me.

worked up to his good knee
seconds and seconds
to make it that far
and holding on the chair
by its seat
hoisted up to his feet

    I'll pick myself up, you—

those words again
the worst

    Pick myself up.
    Pick myself . . .

but I was already
out the back
pushing through
the weeds and dew

Red Clouds

with purple undersides
were lined up
in the west
and moving fast
over the woods

in the last light
the million black
branches of
oak and ash and maple
aspen pine and birch
criss and cross
and cover you
like the ceiling
of the church

I looked up
and there it was
that pinpoint
through the mesh
of black leaves

Rachel and her mother
my mother my father

my father and me
me and whoever
I wanted to fall
into the ground
and not come up

instead I slid
to the bottom
of the slope
where the creek
flowed silver
like a splash
of shiny dimes
over the rocks

I took a step
and crossed the rocks
one by one
to
the other side

I Don't Know Why

maybe to choose
my time
maybe to bail
if I chickened out

but when I went
up the slope
two miles plus
to the churchyard
through the stones
and markers
in the little yard
I went up
heel to toe
and foot by foot
as quiet as I could
until I came to
that little house
his lighted shed

I stood in front
of the wooden door
I stood and stared

it was cross-barred
rough-planked
with different model
hinges and
offset like
my camper doors

and gave off
a slanted
frame of light
around the edge

I stood
and stood

I stood

and when I didn't turn
away
lifted my hand
my knuckles up
and gave the wood
four
knocks

In My Mind

I saw him shiver
in his chair
on the late
October night
so near the graves
of dead church people
his hands frozen
where they sat
one with a pen
one spread across
a sheet of paper

then turn
his wrinkled face
to the door
and wonder
if he heard
four knocks
in the first place

and would God
knock on his door
and why would he
when he

could just float in
or maybe
Death
was calling him
but then
he'd float in too

and not rise
from his chair
but stare at the door
and stare and stare

in my mind
I saw all this

it vanished
when I heard a scrape
of chair legs
on the floor and
a scuffle of shoes
and a click

and then the frame
of light I stood in
was a sudden
door of it

Ah. Ah. Robert, yes?
So late.
Come in.

Robert Lang? Bobby?

he said

    You live down there.
    The green house.

I didn't know
at first how
he knew my name
or house
but he's a priest
so he probably
had some help

yeah
yes

the little churchyard shed
wasn't as small inside
as it looked
still cramped
but not too close

you couldn't walk
the floor

but you could
breathe

    Welcome to my quiet place.
    A little house where
    I think and pray.
    And write.

it was a house
more house than shed
all ink and paper
only ink and paper
but everything
I guess he needed

pictures of God and Jesus
old ones sketched in ink
and pencil
tacked to the walls
between the shelves

which pretty much
were everywhere
and where there were no
shelves there were
stacks of books

books on the desk
filling the seat
of another chair
piled on a stool
stacked on the floor
the rug

the shelf just over his desk
was messy with
lopsided books
where he'd removed
one or two

his desk wasn't a desk
at all
but a table
without drawers
made from a door

the rug under
the table legs
was worn shiny
where his shoes moved

the yellow dome
of the lamp seeped

yellow light on
the yellow pages
some were inked
some were not

How can I help you?

I shrugged my shoulders

I don't know

I *didn't* know how
or why I was even there at all
and wanted suddenly
not to be anywhere
when I heard
my stupid father in my mind

(*You're the reason she left.*)

and how that cut me deep
and also how it cut to see
Jimmy's sagging beer-bottle face
and bony sprawl down
on the kitchen floor
and my mouth said

my father is such a . . . such a . . .

I wanted to swear
but couldn't say the f-word
not here

> *Ah. Well. I haven't seen him*
> *For a while. Years. But I remember him.*
> *He has suffered things, I think.*

and it came out

has he been in jail?
what did he do?

he frowned
like a teacher would
but the frown didn't last

> *Why don't you talk to him?*

so he has been in jail
figures

maybe that's why
he's such an asshole

    Bobby. Bobby.
    Look. It's been forever
    Since I said a word to him.
    Maybe I should check in.
    As a friend?

good luck with that

    Do you want to sit down?

I looked and saw
the stool with
books on top
(fewer than the chair)
I moved them to the floor
and sat

but the moment I did
it seemed so dumb to be there
talking with him
when I don't know how to
that I leaned to leave
ready to bolt

until I saw his papers
the papers on the table
had little drawings
on them

or not drawings
but curly lines
linking these words with those
so many snaky lines
and winding arrows
and tangled threads

he saw me looking
at the nest of papers

Next Sunday's sermon . . .
It's how I write, in little thoughts
That I need to connect to . . . to . . .

and I thought
he was offering me
a look at them
when his head
went down
his chin down
on his chest

and he shook

I should go

    No, no. It's . . . it's just . . .

and he breathed in
sniffed in
and made to pull
a tissue from his pocket
but he didn't find one
and just wiped his nose
on his sleeve

    There is so much hurt in the world,
    Isn't there? I mean, you can hardly
    Not see it.
    Some tragedies we can't help.
    Hurricanes, earthquakes, floods.
    But some we make up
    All by ourselves.
    Bombings, famine, shootings . . .

I'm sorry

    Right. Sorry. We're all sorry, but . . .

I didn't know where
he was going
and luckily he stopped
and found a tissue box

So.
So.

he smiled
an old man smile

That's what all this is.
Trying to be a bit more than sorry.

His Little House

had the smell
of a library like
the library in school
but without the
lunchroom smell

he shifted the papers
together
into something
like a pile

> So tell me about school these days.
> It's been a while since you came to church.
> You're a junior now? Or, no.
> Sophomore.

I should be
but fifth didn't go so well
I'm a freshman

he nodded slowly
then raised his
eyebrows about
something he didn't say

You wanted to talk.
Is it more about your father?

I don't know
not really
I have to go

I got up from the stool

why had I stalked
his little house
and come here anyway?

he stood by the door
not opening it
just stood
and stood

Are you sure there's nothing else?

and they went off
again
my lungs
my breath
my mouth

I Know This Girl

he took his hand
off the handle and
let it fall to his side

Oh. Yes?

she's weird
an artist
really good
but she doesn't like church
or anything really
I don't think she likes me
especially now
but who cares, right?
and anyway
she has a girlfriend
but she really hates her mother

sorry this is all mixed up

but he figured it out

I think I know who you mean.

yeah?
well I don't like my dad
but this girl and her mother
you should hear them

she talks about wanting
her mother
to die
or be gone anyway
I know I shouldn't care but—

    No. You should care.
    Of course you should.

he bit his inside lip

    Good of you to tell me.

well have you seen her drawings?
what she can do?

    I have, yes. Her mother showed me.

you would think
she . . . I mean,
was he messed up?

I pointed to a drawing
he had on his wall
of Jesus with his
crown of thorns on

Jesus? Messed up?

no! the guy who drew him?

Michelangelo?

was he
you know
a perfect saint
or was he mean and . . . whatever?

he snickered a little bit

I read he wasn't all that friendly,
And fairly arrogant,
As maybe a genius might feel
From time to time.
A person with his own agenda, right?
A bit of a bully, I suppose,
So maybe, yes . . .

but the picture is good
isn't it?
it looks good
you have it on your wall

Oh yes. He is
Considered one
Of the finest artists
In history.

she can do that

She can. She could. She's very talented.

but she's
I don't know
mean and snotty
no not snotty
cruel
and she gets mad so fast
it's like
what the hell just happened?

I don't know what to
how to

I can't figure her out

it's only

   Only . . . ?

I took her picture
from inside my jacket
unfolded it on
the table

she did this

he was quiet for a while

   Your face exactly.
   It's you, really.
   It's what I see right now.
   So much going on in there.
   She caught you here.

caught me

that's what she did
that's what I am
caught

She has a lot going on too.

I know
but
I don't know

he laughed

Join the club.

no look
if she's so mean
how can I look
like that to her?
she'll never
really like me
not really
so why?
how?

my heart was pumping loud
blood rushed in my ears
and all my junk
was getting tangled in my head
all knotted up

Rachel her mother
my mother
my father Rachel
junk junk junk

I was sweating
in my shirt
my pants
down my back
ready to say
something I didn't know
a freaking thing about

so I got up
I got up

and those hinges
those mismatched offset hinges squealed
when I pushed
through the door

    Robert, wait.
    Wait.

but I stumbled
down

the dark slope
to the river
to the dark
to my yard
to my other room

I Wired the Doors Shut

wired myself away
from everybody
twisted the wire
in my fingers
until it was tight

wire

wire

I heard they stole a monkey
from its mother
and gave it a mother
made out of wire
instead of a living one
and gave it one
made from towels too

without the living one
it went to the towel one

when they took that away
the monkey had only
the wire mother

it grew up so screwed up
in the head
rocking twitching hiding
and crying
if monkeys even cry

what sort of mother
did I have
for those few months

what kind of father
did she leave me with

what kind of girl
can be so up and down mean
to me

to make me
rock and twitch and hide and cry
like I was doing now

The Picture from the Train

the one she drew
I took it from my coat
and sat up
and stared at it

it stared right back
like it was a mirror
but not the kind of mirror
that showed outside

this one
this one
showed inside enough
for me to almost
not hate this kid
to almost like
this
boy

then the light went off

shut off
just died

I clicked and clicked
the table lamp
tightened the bulb
replugged the cord
but the dark
wouldn't go away

I punched
the pillows
tried to settle down
stayed an hour
in the dark
maybe longer
then unwired the doors
and stormed
across the yard
checking the cords
along the way

until I was inside
in the dark
with only one
stupid candle lit

and him
propped like a dummy

a ghost in clothes
in his chair
his jaw pink
from my knuckle punch

You ungrateful little shit.
I should wallop you
Or turn you in, you bastard—

why don't you?
then I could
go to jail too

Just sit.

no

Sit down.

I had a stupid day

Sit.

there's no power in the bus
it just died
where's the cord?

he followed it with his eyes
to behind the chair

    Sorry.

which is a word
he never used

he bent and plugged
it in and in the yard
the camper windows
lit an amber light

I'm sleeping in the bus

he looked up at me

I'm . . .
I said
sorry I'm sorry

    You're not.

I hated hitting you

anyway that's all
I'm going out

No, that's what I wanted . . .
What I need to talk about
The camper.

it's mine

It's not yours.

it's mine

It's neither of ours
Look. Sit. Let me tell you.

I Was Too Tired to Run

it all leaked out of me
in the quiet
in the room
in the minutes
that came then

him sitting
in his half-stuffed
half-unstuffed
easy chair
shifting his leg
nursing his jaw
with the cold side
of a warm beer

me like a sparrow
rocking
on the bench
by the window
anger swimming
in me but
slowly slowly
swimming off

to somewhere
else

and then I thought
the candlelight was
so I wouldn't see
how hard I'd really hit him
how I'd hurt him

and my chest tightened up
and I choked down
something
but he looked up at me

the flame was low
between us
little sphere of light
round pale moon
shading half
the shadow of his face

and while the pus-white
wax pooled to the rim
of the saucer

the sad black wick like
some last man standing

he used his words

Your Mother

It was hers before,
Long before,
That old camper,
Before we even knew
Each other.

he stuttered this
not looking at me
or anywhere

You won't remember this,
But when there were three
Of us,
You, me, and your mother,
That camper was our world.

his words hung
in the room
held in the dwindling
moon of light
at the center of the table

You were, what,
Not even one? Not six months?

Yeah, this is just before . . .
Well, before I went in.

went in

went in

so her angry mother
was right

it had never been more quiet
than it was then
his voice a whisper
of heels in gravel

> *We drove all over*
> *The west, you laughing or*
> *Talking baby talk*
> *With her in the back*
> *And her pretending*
> *She knew what you meant.*
> *Or both of you in front,*
> *Mommy navigating,*
> *Map in one hand, your*
> *Bottle in the other.*

my arms and legs and neck
no longer rocking
were cased up
in a flesh of ice

I couldn't move
as if spies tapped our
windowpanes
and tried our doors
and any movement
would betray
and mean our death
I was so still

Idaho and Montana,
Down to Utah,
Colorado next,
Then Texas.
She loved those places.
She was from out there, the west.
That's big country
Out there.
Not like here.
And light.
You can't believe how big
Light can be.

the words
his words
as if he'd never spoken
words before
as if these were the first

like Him who spoke
at the beginning
and things became
things
trees wind moon

She had the reddest hair.
I don't know why you don't.
You got my tangly wire.

red hair red hair
and she was suddenly
there with us
like the first stars
must have appeared

so
so how
why did I
make her leave?

You didn't.
You didn't.
God, Bobby, you didn't.
I was just . . . I don't know.
I lied. I lie.
You remind me of me.
And that's what I don't like.
Not you. Me.

a long break
of no words
with just the flame
swaying with
his breath
our breaths

What happened was . . .
I was young. She was young.
Too young.

We had nothing of our own but that camper.
When you came, we practically lived in it.
Driving all over, trying to make it last.
It couldn't last. She loved big country,
But I had family here. Some.
We got this place. She tried but hated it

And wanted to go west again.
We fought. A lot.
I answered that by drinking. Got in bad fights.
It's stupid how you know you're wrecking yourself
but you do it anyway. I stole a car.
Not even a good one, a crap piece of junk.
For the money. Of course I was caught.

Six months.
You were five months old, I guess,
When I went in.

It was hard for her with me inside.
You were a sick little baby.
Ear infections. Bronchitis. Pneumonia once.

my tea bag lungs

When I finally got out, you were in the hospital.
You'd be in there for a week, she said.
Asshole that I was, I got drunk right off
And blamed her for not taking care of you.
Can you freaking believe that? Me blaming her.
We fought. Money. You. Me.
Fighting on the deck for everyone to see.
And then one night I . . .

237

here it is
it's coming

you what—

    I went off my head.
    Blood boiling. Eyes twitching like crazy.
    My hand, my hand, I went to smack her
    Or, I don't know, it looked like I would . . .

    Her face.
    Her beautiful face . . .
    The face I loved so much.

I felt it on my face
whether he did or not
not freezer-cold like
Rachel's mother's slap
but blood-pumping hot

    She backed away from me
    Like a ghost.

    I begged her, but
    She ran out and drove away.

I sat in this hole waiting for her,
Cursing myself to hell.
I knew how stupid I'd been.
All I wanted was to tell her I was sorry,
Tell her I would never
Ever . . .

he was back there
shaking in his mind
for a long
few minutes

Then the police called.
She'd had an accident.
Five miles from here.
She was coming back.

a shiver went
from my feet
to my scalp

an accident in the camper?
in the camper?

but I already knew

the windshield gone
the headlights smashed and gone
the body battered lifeless

I started to cry
he was crying too

    I got so drunk, out of my mind,
    Crawling around, I fell off the freaking deck.
    Broke my leg in three places.
    Cracked my spine.

    You were in foster care
    For a month before
    They let me bring you home.

the room grew smaller
as the flame went down
neither of us wanting
to move to turn on a light

    So that's the mess.
    The whole mess.
    That's why I've been the bum
    Raising you for the last fifteen years.
    You see how that's worked out.

with that he blew out
a long breath
quivering the last
moments of flame

my tongue moved
in the cold dry cave of my mouth

did she
paint
stars on the ceiling
of the bus?

he sobbed out
a hurt wet noise

> *I helped her do that. It was my idea.*
> *She was better at it. So much better.*
> *At everything.*

minutes of quiet
then

> *Long story short, never a day goes by*
> *Without me knowing how I screwed up.*

I did. Not you.
It was never you.

I tried to pull
my mom together
in my mind
red hair
laughing
singing

do you have a picture?

it was a strain
to pull his wallet
from his back pocket

the photo was bad
a cloudy day
far too many mountains
gray and gray and gray
peaking in the back
her red hair flying
and she was too far off
looking down

at a lumpy blanket
in her arms

is that me?

he nodded
as he took the photo back
pressed it
to his chest
where
his breaths
came ragged and wet

> *Mommy . . .*
> *Mommy was a funny lady.*
> *You don't know how funny.*
> *And she sang*
> *To keep me from falling*
> *Asleep on the long*
> *Straight roads out there.*
>
> *She wouldn't let me sing*
> *When she drove, though.*
> *I have no voice.*

But her . . .
She always sang the sad ones.

"Love is like a fading ember . . ."

his hollow voice
almost without
tone almost

dying

    What?

the word is dying *ember*
you listen to it enough

    See. I can't even get that right.

is that why you listen
to the slow sad stuff

because of her?

he raised his eyes
from the almost vanished flame

Pathetic, isn't it.

no not really I thought
and then I went

take me down
where the trains run slow

and he met my eyes
and sighed out
a long long breath
and said

    My hair, yeah.
    But you got her voice.

I Unplugged

the camper cord
from the wall
moved to the couch
and lay in the dark
the longest time
smelling candle smoke

I'd taken all this in
his story of our past
just watching him
staring I guess

hearing in my mind
him try to sing
in the camper
with me and mom
her stopping him
and all that western light

dad's eyes had closed
I closed mine too
to get it blank
inside

and waves of
I don't know what
kind of wind
went through me
as if I was a tree
and all my limbs
and leaves
were moving
humming
floating on
the breathing of the air

and while the air
breathed
and he breathed
and I breathed
I fell inside
myself
to sleep

Some Mornings

as much as I need
the night and dark
to drape
over me
like a cape of iron

the lightness of the light
lifts me some mornings
to a place where
I can stand
myself

and just forget for a while
all the junk I trip over
the knots I'm twisted in

I even fake a
glance in the mirror
without seeing me

some mornings early
I could come down and
he was already
at the radio

Baby, it'll be all right.

it'll be all right
it'll be
it'll be all right

and maybe
if you suck in
a breath and
count to five
in the time it takes to
count to ten
but take it slow and
only count to five you can

just

get

out

the

door

and that's what I did

Except It Wasn't All Right

Rachel rushed at me
in the hall
within ten minutes
of me getting there

she came at me
at no one else
the hall was moving and moving
bodies crossing
all those faces
voices
but of them all
she came at me

look, I didn't mean—
I started
about holding her hand
I know you like Maggi—

but then she coughed out
gargled out
hissed out
that her mother

—told Maggi's parents!

told them about what
the girls had been up to
dating
kissing
and whatever
told them what they *were*

> Maggi said her parents weren't
> Even mad at her.
> They thought my mother was
> A total lunatic.
> They said she was too young
> To know if she was gay.
> As if!
> She's as gay as gay
> And knows it.
> They told her I'm unstable
> And weird.

my tongue moved
in my mouth
but my lips went tight
and wouldn't work

> Then they tried to tell her
> I was using her.
> That I forced myself on her.

Forced!
Can you believe it?
If they say anything to ruin my chance
To go to the academy—

I don't think they—

I need to get out of here.
I swear I'll . . . I'll . . .

what
what will you do

Then they told her,
Told Maggi,
Made her
Break it off with me.

and?

and?

And she did.

Then Rachel Asked Me

to come over
after school

except she didn't ask
she really said

    Come over.

it wasn't an ask
like none of her
asks were asks

    My mother's home.
    She's there.
    I can't be alone with her.
    That face looking at me.
    I need someone there.
    Come over. That's all.
    Come over.

she hates me
she hates me more than anything

    She's full of it.
    Besides, she's probably cooking up

Something sneaky,
Which maybe she won't if you're there.
Anyway, what do you care?
I need somebody there.

she looked
like she would
just go up in flames
right in the hall
so I broke my rule and said

okay

I'd take
the bus home
with her

As If They Doubled

the length of the day
it went on forever

I had hours and hours
to think of ways
to say no way

but every time I saw her face
and it was always there
her iron twitching eyes
were like a flicking lighter
near a spill of gasoline
that soaked me too

what could I do
what could I make different
what
what
who am I
to go or not to go

and there she was
at the final bell
flicking clicking

and there I was
on her bus
the whole thing
crashing in my head
like the thousand plates
my mother threw

too soon too soon
the bus slowed
near her house

she jumped up from our seat
stomped up the aisle
and stopped dead
on the bus stairs
staring down

She Stopped Dead on the Stairs

when she saw him
standing near a tree
waiting at her stop

Father Percy

    No, God, no.

she said

    Guys?

the driver said

he stretched his hand to the door lever
his eyes on me
as if (ha) I was the normal one

    Rachel?

the priest said

    Miss, come on.

she jumped to the ground
both feet together
as if to pound
a hole in it

I followed
and the door whooshed closed

       Rachel?

Father Percy said

and she said like a spit

    You! I'm not talking to you.

then to me
to me she said

    You knew he'd be here, didn't you?

what?
no—

she stormed away
but the priest kept on

and caught up to her
arms hands reaching out

he didn't touch her
(oh please don't)
but she shook her
shoulders loose
as if he had

I heard from ten paces
eight paces five
stumbling to keep up

she had forgotten about me
that's fine
I heard her anyway
and him

and what he said
in his slow low words
that landed
like a printed page

> *Rachel, please,*
> *I wonder if we can chat,*
> *Just a few words about—*

he glanced aside at me

>   —*what might be going on.*
>   *I think if we could talk.*
>   *Your mother's worried and so am—*

she turned
whirled on her heels
and faced him
with her face
more mad and mean than
ever

>   *My mother! My mother can go to hell*
>   *If she thinks I'm going straight,*
>   *And you can too.*
>   *Both of you!*

both?
me too?

and then

she swore at him
and wouldn't stop

and kept on
right there on the street
at him
her mother
and the world

        Rachel, listen—

his hand tugged at his neck
and a strip of white
slid out of his black collar

        Not as a priest.
        Not as anyone but a friend.

    I don't care.

then I said
Father, tell her you don't want to change her
Rachel, listen—

but she ran and ran
leaving me with him
his feet planted on the lawn
somebody's lawn

all blood gone
from his features

he stood dumbstruck so
I managed to say
she thinks you want to make her
not be gay

Father shook his head

> *No, that's . . . no . . .*
> *That, that . . . I can't care about that.*
> *It's the anger, the blindness*
> *Hurting the two of them.*
> *I'm worried,*
> *You're worried, I know you are,*
> *Because you care.*

he tried to spot her down the street
but she wasn't there

> *I'll find a way to talk with her,*
> *With both of them. But*
> *Will you go after Rachel? Now?*
> *Bobby, would you do that?*

me? I . . .

I . . . guess

      She trusts you, I think,
      And shouldn't be alone.

I don't know

maybe

okay

      Thank you, Bobby.

I did go
to the house I knew was hers
yellow like a buttery sun
blue door
flowers bunching around the lamppost
and took a step up
the walk from the street

but suddenly I felt like rags inside
like I'd been shredded up
too much by everything

by all her razor blades
and so I turned

maybe I heard some tapping
on a window
maybe not
but I wasn't there
long enough to hear

I Had to Be Alone

had to sew the ragged shreds
back in place
quiet the clattering crashing clanging
in my head

because it's me
it's me
my life
whatever it is or isn't
I sure don't need this

I mean why was it always
up and down with her
and close and far
okay and weird
and friend not friend?

it made me sick
it made me want to sleep
it made me want to
be somewhere else

Don't touch me, you freak!

the word slapped
like a ruler slapping sunburn

Freak!

well I knew that
and worse much worse
but did she have to say it?

why had she drawn me
so I didn't look half-bad?

and her swearing at the priest
holy shit this sad old man
who cried from floods
and hungry babies

I didn't know
I didn't know
what to think
say
do
be

I went to my camper
and slammed the doors

and tried to shut off
my head
my face
my eyes
my breath

I Stripped the Picture

from the wall
where I had taped it up

it stared at me
under the light
like I stare at faces
and make people mad

and

I still didn't get
how she could
do it
make it live
like a real thing
just out of lines and lines
seen by her eyes

her eyes

her eyes could
somehow see a me
that is more me
than I am

that is so weirdly more
so better than
actual
me

how do you deal
with that?

and more than that
what was this kid

this boy

myself

what was I going to
say
do
be?

How Long I Was There

before the camper doors
cracked and slivered open
I couldn't say

it woke me up

not now, dad, go away—

but the fingers were not his
they were long and charcoal-stained
and shaking
as they unwired the wire
until the doors pulled back
and night came in

as if opening a passage
to a tomb
the night came in

and like the night herself
she crawled in next to me

    I'm going to do it.
    Tonight.

do what?
I said then said
you know, never mind
I don't like you right now

    I'm going to do something.
    To get back.

she was breathing hard
as if she'd run away
from home
her clothes
stank of cigarettes

    I am.

who cares?
not me
I don't care

then she smiled
one of those smile-less smiles
and tossed a bag
of chips at me
and when I wouldn't
touch it split it

open and set it
on my chest
like freaking boyfriend girlfriend
and picked at it

you hate me
remember?

    I hate everybody.

she snickered

then I said
he doesn't hate you

a pause a long one

    Maybe.
    But no one listens to me.

because all you do is swear

another wait then

    Look. I'm sorry I called you that.
    Freak. I'm one too.
    You know that, right?

not buying it
lame just lame

Wait. You still have this thing?

she snatched the picture
from the floor next to me
and stuck it straight up
among those stars

then she flicked her lighter
thumb-turned a dial to spear the flame
up high
shining those stars
and the ceiling
of my whole metal room
glowed with the stars
my mother painted there
my parents painted there
with me in the middle

that's when I saw
how Rachel's cheeks
were wet and red

what happened?

and her face went
to stone

> *She won't let up.*

you should just go talk to him

> *She pushed me too far this time.*

you're not listening

> *Too far.*

what
did she hit you
what did she—

Jimmy yelled out from the house

> *Hey, Bobby. Another picture!*
> *Bobby? You out there?*
> *It's Mommy. A photo.*

I sat up

you need to sort this out
not me
I have to go

    No.

you're too much
I have—

    What? You have what?

I'm going in

she growled and sat up
next to me

    Gah! I'm out of here.

The Shriek

the camper doors made
when her palms
double-pushed the two of them apart

was like a screaming bird
an angry wounded bird
thrashing in the leaves

and she flew out
into the night
as cold and quick and dark
as the cold dark air

Rachel—
I said

but she was gone

I Don't Know Why

I followed her

Why did you follow her?

I don't know why
I followed her
but I did
like she dragged me
in her screaming wake

it was hard going
down the slope
there was no moon
the sky was low
and black with
a smell of cold
and every step
a half slip

she sloshed
almost like a drunk
across the creek
and up the other side
toward the church

at every step and stumble
I shouted
at myself to not
go after her
she's a messed-up jerk
whatever she does
she does

I called out
come on wait
where are you going?

she only went faster
as if she were either
trying to get
away from me
or coax me after

what are you even doing?

a weird noise from
her
a crazy kind of laugh
like a devil
spewing her plan
in a single word

Burn!

burn?

burn what?

His Little House

his yellow light
the pinhole light
was suddenly a beacon
in the dark

she scrambled
through the trunks
and leaves
and tangled growth
up the valley side

Rachel, stop—

but already she was
near the top
already hovering outside
the little window
looking in

   It's empty. Good.

come on
he's not against you
he doesn't even care

she tugged hard on
the shed's door handle
it wasn't locked

we need to get out of here

she looked inside
at the stacks and stacks
of books on shelves
on the table
on the floor

the pictures pinned
to the walls
all those faces of Jesus

and on the table
little lines of ink on pages
and a stack of white
clean paper not yet pages
a lumpy vase
of pens and pens

she saw it all
everything I saw

but the anger
was hers alone

    Look at this.
    He's probably writing
    About me.

you're an idiot
he doesn't care
you know he's all right
we need to leave

    What are you, his weird little altar boy?

her dark side came quick and quicker
she flicked the lighter
and a tongue of flame
popped high
like a ghost
freed from
his stony tomb

get—out—of—here!

and just like with my dad
my skinny stick arms

jolted alive and I pushed her
out the door

touched pressed grabbed her
roughly this time

    What the hell!
    I wasn't going to—

she fell and her hand
her hand
her iron hand
went back
the lighter flame still on

it was so fast

the trees meshed for days overhead
had kept it all so dry

the brittle leaves
were hungry and went up too fast to stop

she screamed
and edged away

I stomped at leaves and leaves
tried to kick them down
but they were alive
full of themselves

kick them away from the house!

but she was useless
crying spinning
looking for something

a broad thick layer
of leaves caught then
drifting lifting
near his little house

I tore my jacket off
and swatted at the flames
they splashed my hands
boiling and freezing them

Help! Help!

she cried out
in a voice so weak
it made me mad

flames scratched at
the shed
the shed boiled alive
like water rolling up
so quick so quick

Rachel, help me stop it!

then *he* yelled
Father Percy
from the churchyard
and his huffing
running
thumping
across the ground

> *Oh my Lord!*
> *Oh dear God!*
> *Oh!*
> *Oh no!*

Then Not Just Him

but I thought God
Himself must
be stomping down to us

everything at once
turned silver
in the world
the air the sky
my hands
the fire
her face

like someone stabbed
me through the eyes

and silver cut
a sliver in the sky
sliced it up
and down
and wind
and freezing rain
poured down the air
rushing at
the tiny two of us

as though the girders
holding heavy heaven
high up there
buckled like the joists
holding up
a moldy ceiling
and dropped
the whole weight
of its weight on us

lightning
thunder
and rain came down
and rain and rain and rain

She Ran Away

I ran for
her
leaving my
self
behind
following again

Rachel!

not even thinking
that by calling her
now Father Percy
would know it was
Rachel by her name
and me by calling her

she flew back up the slope and
was twisting like her own storm
halfway down the trail
where I saw her
stumbling forward at top speed

stop! Rachel stop!

my fingers burned
as if I'd stuck them in a socket
as if my bones
were razor wire

the sudden rain was cold
and blinding
stinging my hands
until I finally reached her
two point three miles
from my house

where she was like a ghost
standing
leaning out
on that foundation
slab of brick and stone
over the steepest drop
in the woods

she was looking down

I stopped short

Rachel . . .

she turned to me
her face in the sudden lightning
red and wet
from rain and tears
hair plastered on
her forehead
her eyes black holes
her skin chalky white

It's Over Now

she screamed into the rain

I'm done. Nothing.
Nothing.

it's not over
nothing
is over

I thought the rain
might stop his quiet house
from burning
but the flames kept rising up
I heard sirens now

get away from the edge
and stop running away

her voice then
was a scratch of glass

I don't want to do this anymore.

then her voice went low
as if she was possessed

I've screwed up everything.
If I can't do my art,
I don't want anything.

don't you dare!
Rachel—

I went to her
step by slow step
not knowing what
to do
or say
or be
to get her off
that ledge of stone

I went to her
my arms
my hands to her

too late

her feet

moved

She Fell

leaving the stone
brick concrete
slab foundation

except she didn't fall

she flew

some angle of replay might
show she
slippedwalkeddroppedjumpedthrewherself
straight off that edge of stone

into the mouth
of it
the valley
the pit
the hole

and thunder came
and came and came

I Trippedrolleddivedtoppleddown

the slope my legs going out
two random sticks
under me
sliding pinging ponging
to where I heard her
body crash and crack
and snap
and break
against the trees
and rocks
and splashy ground

thuds yells screams
and sudden silence
as if the sky pulled back
its own wild storm
for one short second

and all there was
was the silence of
her dead at the bottom

then

A Wail

like some sick
sickening moan
some dying
bear horse bird man

and in a spark of lightning
I saw her
bent on the rocks
below

I fell to her
crawled to her
cut my face
my lip in half
banged up my knees

her face slipped facedown
in the water
her short hair
slick to her head
was all I saw

Rachel!

I pulled
her shoulders up
I didn't know
I didn't know
but she would drown
if I didn't move her

    just don't don't don't

I slipped my
puppet arms
and stinging burning hands
under her back
and picked her
stumbling up
from the water
and wrestled her

step by step
foot by foot
up the slope
to the trail

you never know
how you do things
you just do them

in my head was
get up to the trail
up to the trail
only to the trail
just do it do it

and I did

Then I Carried Her

I carried her
my wire arms on fire
my fingers screaming
my lips bleeding
down my chin
eyes stinging
from smoke
and ash
and freezing rain
to the mouth
of the trail

you . . . you're . . .

yeah
I know
a loser freak
shut up

down the street to
the nearest house
I laid her carefully
on the lawn

threw a stick at
the front door
and ran into the woods

I heard them rush outside
see the flames
through the rain-swaying branches
then spot the crumpled
girl twisting on the lawn

the wife ran back inside
to make the call

the husband heard my rustling
in the trees
and ran after me

so that is why

all that is why

I ran I fled I crept away

to hide

Mom's Camper

was the first place
they would look

so it was hardly hiding

but I felt safe
in those snug walls
closed up in there
the light not on
and only
painted stars
to show
my better face
was looking
down at me

I saw the flames
from the window
and the black shapes
of firefighters
moving in front
like a movie
that was like
no movie

I could have run
but could not move
I guess I wanted
to be found
expected
to be found

hoped I'd
be found

I was

Banging Brought Me Out

and the screaming
of Rachel's mother
and the cops
and my dad

they found me
where I hid
but did not hide

Jimmy standing staring
from the yard
a thousand questions
on his face

her mother shrieking

You were there!
You were there!

Mrs. . . . Please . . .

that was some cop
who turned to me and said

Son, there is a girl
Hurt,
And a burning shed.

his quiet house
I know

Did you . . .

I was there
for both

Bobby, don't say anything!

Is that your father?

yes

Then come with us, please,
Both of you.

They Drove Us

to the station
the police station

where a nurse
cleaned me up
my hands and face
and lips

and all the while
my mind was
a whirling blank
of nothing useful
except one thing
one thing
I knew that I would do

Jimmy like a tv dad
asked for a lawyer right off
then twisting like I've never seen him
leaned on a desk
shaking his head
not saying much
confused

we waited there
sitting standing staring
not talking
waiting waiting
my lips zipped up
all by themselves
and wouldn't let me speak
while we waited there

and while we waited
a policewoman came in
holding a plastic bag
inside the bag
Rachel's burned-up lighter

then Father Percy
came running in
my heart spiked
because I didn't know
how much he'd seen
of what happened
at the shed

before the lawyer came
Father Percy asked to talk
to the policewoman

she said her name
I didn't get it
they spoke for a bit
low words
then he looked at me
and took me to an office
that was empty
we sat down

   All right, Bobby, look.
   I don't know what you're planning to say, but—

it's my fault

he took a breath
and pressed his lips tight
then dragged his chair
across the rug right up to me
two jerky lines
through the neat
vacuum stripes
while the cops
and Jimmy
and Rachel's mother
waited

and sat facing me
his legs pumping up and down
his hands trembling
his eyes red
ash on his black shirt
soot on his cheeks
cuts on his hands
almost nose to nose
with me whispering

> *Robert, I was there.*
> *I saw most of it.*

it's still my fault

> *Is it?*

you didn't see you don't know
I pushed her out of the shed
and and
and pulled her lighter from her
and
threw it in the leaves

> *Bobby—*

which caught fire
which they wouldn't have done
if I hadn't
so . . .

Father Percy leaned back
from my nose
he puffed coffee
breath from his mouth

> *She asked for me*
> *To come to the hospital.*

tell me she'll be all right

he said she broke three ribs
one arm and busted up
her leg and messed
both hands and fingers
nothing fatal
but I cried
to think of her banged up
so bad

then he said again

She asked for me to come.

which by some miracle
I knew what he meant

confession

had she told him
what she went there for?
had she told him everything?

they have the lighter
even if they can't tell whose it is
they know somebody started the fire

It was an accident.

that's not true!
besides

Besides what?

I don't know

So what are you going to do?
Make it easier for her by lying?

Saying you did it. Have this
On your record?

no
I don't know
maybe
who cares?

I care. Your father cares.
Rachel. She cares.

good one.

Look, it's my property anyway.
Not church property,
The shed.
I built it myself.
So it's my call,
And I say it wasn't either of you.

they won't believe it

I went out to have a smoke,
Saw you, was surprised,
and dropped my lighter.

I don't know exactly, but I won't let
This go the wrong way.

shouldn't you ask the Pope
if it's okay to lie?

Robert, don't.

I have to say something
I have to speak up

he stood from his chair
sat down again

You do, you absolutely do, Bobby, yes.
And you have. To me.
But it's not Christ you're speaking to in the station tonight,
Not someone who sees all the way into your heart.
It's busy, tired people who can't see inside you,
Who can't, because maybe you won't let them.

and you can?
see inside?

he breathed again
sat back leaned forward

was going to say
something
but I did

what she can do
that's . . .
she needs to do it
to keep doing it

he shook his head once
looked out the door
of the office
to the others
a new man stood with them
the lawyer

Rachel saw me
like I don't see myself
maybe she's the one
who really has soft eyes

he raised his face to me

You were listening.

I listen
I see stuff

    I know you do.
    You see everything.
    And you let her in, not an easy thing to do.
    You are her friend.

he went quiet
for a minute

    And the other part, what will you say
    About how she ended up down by the river?

I looked at him
into his eyes as
he looked into mine

she said some bad things
on the ledge
it's all over I can't live
stuff like that

    Rachel will need to talk to someone.
    I will do everything in my power
    To help her.

then
I guess

I'll tell the truth

    Which is?

that it was
raining lightning thundering

it was crazy in the woods

and she

slipped

he swallowed
nodded his head slowly
breathed out again
again

    All right, then. Come on.
    And after this, let's rebuild the shed
    Together, you and me.

but

But nothing.
Let's talk to them now.
The police, your father,
Everyone.
Okay?

it was hard to make
my mouth move
and there was nearly
no air coming up
my throat
but I said

okay
yeah
yes

So I Said No Way

did she set any fire
I was there and saw she didn't

there was a storm
there was a fire
everything was sudden
too sudden to see right

and she only tripped and fell
in the stormy woods
while she ran for help

Father Percy told them

> *I went out there for a break.*
> *The children surprised me.*
> *I dropped my lighter.*
> *Rachel ran for help.*
> *Robert followed her.*

they wrote this down

> *And why did you want to speak*
> *With Robert Lang just now?*

Because I am his priest.

Jimmy didn't blink

And I am his friend.

her mother was a mess
but since there
were no other witnesses
and one of the ones
who said he saw it all
was a priest

that ended it

The Art School Said

that they would take her still
they would admit her
the moment
her ribs
and arms and legs
and hands healed up enough
for her to take her lessons

If you can't make
First semester,
You can do second.
And the summer session too.
Your work is too good
To let this slow you down.

I liked that they knew it
and said it
because it was true

and if she was
broken inside
like her body was
for weeks after that night

maybe she could
sometime
somewhere
unbreak herself

It Stormed

for weeks
first rain
then snow
then rain
and thunderstorms
all of that month
a kind of gray

even after Rachel
came back to school
the big part of it
was over
my part

except for maybe
seeing her limping
around the halls
which because of how
I always saw her face
was hard not to do

some days a car
came to take her out
before the school day ended

Mondays was her mother
Thursdays just a car

    Therapist

she mouthed to me in the hall
one time
I did the same

good for you

but it was weird
she knew I knew she had confessed
I knew she knew I lied for her

I felt every eye was watching us
and stayed away from her

which was sort of like before
folding myself in myself
mope the halls
keep
my eyes down
count my strides
feel my way

to corners
count the doors
fountains and lavs
all without looking up

until one time I turned my
face a little to the left
and there she was

her eyes drawing me
to her
catching me
cornering me
in the art room hall

I'm going to the city tomorrow.
Come see me off.

Jimmy Didn't Speak

when he took me
to the train station

she was there with
her mother
her father would be waiting
at the other end

she stood on the platform
one arm in a sling
moving stiffly
like some half-dead soldier
her black case resting
at her side

her mother stepped
away
didn't look at me
but didn't scream
at me either

progress
I thought

I'll split my time—

she said
starting as usual
in the middle of a thought

she was talking about
life and her new school
which had started her
in weekend classes

nodding backward
she whispered

> *We talk. The three of us. A lot.*
> *He's smart, your priest. The therapist too.*
> *My mother promised not*
> *To make my life*
> *A living hell.*

things are looking up

> *Ha. Yeah. Maybe because*
> *Of him. Maybe because*
> *She almost lost me.*
> *Hilarious, huh?*

yeah
yeah but
not so much

she chewed her lip
looked at her mother then
at me

> *So I'll be here part-time*
> *Part-time with my dad.*
> *I have a therapist there too.*
> *It's better.*
> *We'll see what happens.*

her mother was getting all
twitchy
pacing up and back
until the train came
running slow
until it stopped

that was pretty much it
except Rachel hugged me
not long but
yeah

after that
her mother disappeared
as if no one there

and Jimmy snickered
from where he stood
leaning against the truck

> *She's some piece of work,*
> *The mother, yeah?*

yeah

but there was
a look on his face
I've never seen before

I stepped away from
the truck
to see him better
like the art teacher
at the art taped up
that day it all began

it was like for the first time
dad wasn't squinting

from a hangover
no he was just aching from
his leg and back

I think I'll walk

I said

he nodded like
a cowboy
just the once

    Go for it.

I walked the long way home
trying to get myself back
to myself
in the woods
in the trees
but not
not really
not really able to

It Hurt How Many

trees had fallen
in the storms
toppled cracked jagged off
from their trunks
dismembered
on the ground

some in a final huddle
hiding from the fury
some stark alone
bleeding black water

ash oak and maple

like bodies wrecked
and flung
in ditches
on some battlefield
down south

sure more light came
down onto the trail
joggers doggers bikers
would love that

when I got near home
I saw the mossy roof
of our dark house
now even had
a splash of gold
across the shingles

it would be there
for an hour in the morning
from the hole where
some tree used to be

but living things
had died
for all that light
aspen pine birch
oak and ash and maple

it presses on your heart
like the heel
of someone's iron glove
to see a thing
so tall reaching from
deep under us
to the big wide blue
now lying twisted there
split

amputated
stock-still
no life
no breath
all wrong

branches and sticks
scattered everywhere
along the trail
just lying where they lie

there is no putting
a tree back up after
it's broken
and fallen
in a storm

maybe with us
with people
it's different
maybe

I Thought

of Rachel gone
and it was fine
good
good enough

quieter

time would go by
as it was passing
in the woods

all the final leaves
would fall
the sticks would fall
I'd walk the trail
as slow as I could walk

I found after a while
the questions
in my head
were mostly mine

and this over all the others

Rachel,
can I tell you
one last thing?

I Thought I Was

okay living
with a wire dad
a stick dad
who had
fallen only near
to me

I'd lived
that way
for years
so I was doing fine

me a single
thing alone
motherless
not slow maybe
but not quick either
who tried to not care less
about whatever

then you busted in
forced your way in me
like you busted in
the camper that night

I thought I was junk
until I saw your drawing
of me

I thought I saw things
but you see things too

you saw a thing
beneath
my face my look
it wasn't normal no
so far from normal
but not junk either

you can do a lot
you could listen more
get out of your own head
but you can do a lot
so much more than most

so

go

please

and do the thing that
makes you do it

just go and do it

when that was out
when I had got that out
the words I'll tell her
someday soon
whatever they might mean
the trail went quiet
my head
my jumping heart
went quiet
as quiet
as I needed them
to be

The First Thing I Saw

when I made it out back
was a can of soda
on the roof
of the camper bus

then Jimmy moved
half-in half-out
the driver's door
spray cleaner in his hand

half a dozen
empty tins of motor oil
and three five-gallon
tanks of gasoline
two gleaming headlights
with their wires to the sky
were sprawled
across the ground
like the remains
of a party

the engine panel
in the rear
was tipped up

kneeling under it
his hands deep inside
the motor guts
was Ray

his wife's legs
bent out from under
the bus
both knees up
as she clanked and swore
something sharp
and Ray laughed

Shh. The kid.

dad turned
and nodded
his chin at me

I came over

what's all this?
what are you doing?

my chest filling
with hot dripping
salt water

Dad?

he gave me then
a wrinkled smile
nodding and nodding
as he fished for words
while my heart sank
and rose
and my veins
went cold as ice

     June.

he said

just

     June.

That's All He Said

June? what about June?

   After it's all done.

what are you talking about?

   After school is done.
   After you rebuild his house.
   We'll go. I'll pick you up.
   Maybe on the last day.
   And we'll go.

where?

   Denver.
   Salt Lake.
   Idaho.
   I don't know.
   Wherever.

I stared at his face
it didn't sag
from too much beer

his eyes were on me
watching my forehead
the muscles around
my eyes
my mouth
taking me in

To all those states she loved.

and the soaking lump
inside my chest
my throat
pushed up into my eyes
I wiped my face
on my sleeve

really?

You can navigate.
I need you . . . to help me do that.

Anyway, we'll do our best.
Hell, I don't know if we can even
Find those places again
After all these years.
But we can try.

And you should see them.
She'll be there, a part of her.

and I shivered
to my toes
and felt like falling
down in tears

which like they planned it
was when Mrs. Ray
leaned in the cabin door
and turned the key
and Ray stood back
and the engine's
wheels and belts
exploded
with a haze of blue

it coughed and sputtered
then seemed to die

then caught again

and the whole bus
quaked to life
jiggling

on its cinder blocks
near the edge of the woods
in the back of the yard
at the end of the trail

then Jimmy slapped
me lightly on the arm
and pointed to
the nowhere road

where his weekday
beer guy Mike
was driving in
with four more or less
usable tires
bulging from his
bungee-corded trunk

I Almost Cried

right then and there

no way was dad
a wire dad
I couldn't say that now

maybe a stick
but if he was one
then I was too

either way
storm or no storm
we were together

two things
in the same place
at the same time

so

good for us

Behind the Church

the planks I hadn't
thrown away
those cleaned-up
two-by-fours
I spent hours on
were what we'd use
to frame the shed

my father had driven
them over and
dropped them off
one morning
without telling me

Father Percy's back
was to me when
I came up through
the woods
that first day

one hand on his hip
a hammer hanging from the other
he'd already cleared away
the old studs and boards

and cleared the floor
which we would use
because it was intact

he heard me
through the brush
turned his head
I stopped
didn't know what
to say
so he said

    Look at this.

and went to a stump
where a big envelope sat

he slipped out a
heavy sheet of paper
with tissue taped
over it

    She drew it for me.
    For my wall.
    For when we finish this.

it was exact
the Michelangelo
the face of Jesus
with his crown
and his eyes that
looked inside your heart

my chest ached
like that first time
I saw her art

she saw that picture
for half a second
not even that long
we were hardly
in the door before
I pushed her out . . .

But she caught it, his face,
Jesus, with all the sorrow and glory
Of that small moment
When He looks at you. It's here.
It's what she found in you
On the train.
This is her gift.

if she uses it right
maybe

> *Instead of being a forger,*
> *Which she could be, I think.*

he snorted
a laugh
probably wanted
me to join him
but I couldn't
I was crying inside

> *Are you excited about your trip?*

trip?

> *Out west.*

how did you know about that?

> *Your father. We've talked a bit.*
> *Not much. A little.*

it stunned me
that my father

would talk
and now I almost couldn't

    You did a decent thing.
    A kind thing.
    She has a long road, yes,
    But this, this talent
    Will help, I think.
    We need this beauty now.
    She's beyond good, really.

he put the drawing
back in the envelope
on the stump

I still couldn't
say a word

    We won't talk
    If you don't want to.
    No questions to answer
    If you don't want.
    Just work.

and some weight
the leaden heavy thing

of fifteen years
floated off
my shoulders
like a drift of smoke
in the light coming
down from the trees

I gave him a nod
and as much of a smile
as I could manage

and we set to work

Author's Note

I have always felt sympathy for the young person, usually a boy, who may not feel adequate to the demands of the world he finds himself in. It seems to speed around him, blurring his ability to take hold of it. He is quiet, unsure most of the time, and though he can be thoughtful, kind, creative, and imaginative, these attributes are not always helpful when dealing with others. Robert Lang is such a boy, not the first in my books.

In looking into Robert's life, I found Rachel Braly moving into my mind and taking up residence, too. I'm happy to know her and love her just as much. Together, these two outliers share a part, a small part, of their story with us. If reading about others broadens our physical universe, it also inspires our mental lives. Getting to know fictional selves can help us build—and build up—sensors that alert us to the nuances of what the actual people around us say, or do not say, about themselves, and helps us to deal with them.

It's no secret that people are complex, inconsistent, and difficult, and they suffer depression, isolation, family tension:the whole spectrum of human emotion. So, if you see something or hear something that doesn't seem right, if you *don't* see or hear what you think you should, even if you simply *feel* something—share it. Our world is one of undeniable beauty and unavoidable risk. We are in it together, each of us a single instrument in a vast symphony. We're here to play our parts.

Some resources for readers who want to know more about these issues include the Suicide Prevention Resource Center (www.sprc.org), which contains information about how to recognize depression, alienation, bullying, and other causes of teen suicide, and what to do when you see someone at risk. The National Domestic Violence Hotline (www.thehotline. org) has resources for those suffering or suspected of suffering violence at home, including a Chat Now feature in English and Spanish and manned hotlines at 1-800-799-7233 and 1-800-787-3224 (TTY). The American Society for the Positive Care of Children (www.americanspcc.org/bullying-and-schools) offers help in situations of bullying behavior. Naturally, these are only a few of the many resources available. Closer to home, of course, are trusted parents, teachers, counselors, clergy, and, in some cases, the police, all of whom can be expected to help with such issues.

I want to thank, as always, my wife and my daughters for

their constant support of my strange vocation of writing about people they haven't met. Nora Raleigh Baskin was critical and so kind in responding to my first drafts of this story; your faith, Nora, helped me let these characters speak their hearts. Katherine Tegen, being edited so sensitively and persuasively by you has been an honor. Your talent for shaping a difficult story has helped take the manuscript to a far higher level from where it started. I am grateful to Sara Schonfeld for her thoughtful commentary on critical passages; her keen eye and love of the characters have made their story much stronger. My thanks to Jen Strada, whose many microtonal suggestions so enhanced the music of Bobby's narration, and to Anna Prendella for her substantive editorial remarks throughout. I continue to be thankful to Patricia Reilly Giff, who got me started on this wonderful journey so many years ago. Cheers to you all.

TONY ABBOTT is the author of many books for young readers, including the series the Secrets of Droon and the Copernicus Legacy and the novels *Firegirl*, *Lunch-Box Dream*, *The Great Jeff*, and *Denis Ever After*. Tony has worked in libraries and bookstores and at a publishing company and has taught creative writing. He has two grown daughters and lives in Connecticut with his wife and two dogs. You can visit him online at www.tonyabbottbooks.com.